The *Oxford Progressive English Readers* series provides a wide range of reading for learners of English.

Each book in the series has been written to follow the strict guidelines of a syllabus, wordlist and structure list. The texts are graded according to these guidelines; Grade 1 at a 1,400 word level, Grade 2 at a 2,100 word level, Grade 3 at a 3,100 word level, Grade 4 at a 3,700 word level and Grade 5 at a 5,000 word level.

The latest methods of text analysis, using specially designed software, ensure that readability is carefully controlled at every level. Any new words which are vital to the mood and style of the story are explained within the text, and reoccur throughout for maximum reinforcement. New language items are also clarified by attractive illustrations.

Each book has a short section containing carefully graded exercises and controlled activities, which test both global and specific understanding.

The War of the Worlds

H.G. Wells

Hong Kong
Oxford University Press
Oxford

Oxford University Press

Oxford   New York
Athens   Auckland   Bangkok   Bombay
Calcutta   Cape Town   Dar es Salaam   Delhi
Florence   Hong Kong   Istanbul   Karachi
Kuala Lumpur   Madras   Madrid   Melbourne
Mexico City   Nairobi   Paris   Singapore
Taipei   Tokyo   Toronto

and associated companies in
Berlin   Ibadan

Oxford is a trade mark of Oxford University Press

Copyright by the Literary Executors of the Estate of H.G. Wells
This adaptation first published 1992
This impression (lowest digit)
3   5   7   9   10   8   6   4

© Oxford University Press 1992

Not for sale in the UK or Republic of Ireland

All rights reserved. No part of this publication may be reproduced,
stored in a retrieval system, or transmitted, in any form or by any means,
without the prior permission in writing of Oxford University Press
(China) Ltd. Within Hong Kong, exceptions are allowed in respect of any
fair dealing for the purpose of research or private study,
or criticism or review, as permitted under the Copyright Ordinance
currently in force. Enquiries concerning reproduction outside
these terms and in other countries should be sent to
Oxford University Press (China) Ltd at the address below

This book is sold subject to the condition that it shall not, by way of
trade or otherwise, be lent, re-sold, hired out or otherwise circulated
without the publisher's prior consent in any form of binding or cover
other than that in which it is published and without a similar condition
including this condition being imposed on the subsequent purchaser

Illustrated by K.Y. Chan

Syllabus designer: David Foulds

Text processing and analysis by Luxfield Consultants Ltd

ISBN 0 19 585466 7

Printed in Hong Kong
Published by Oxford University Press (China) Ltd
18/F Warwick House East, Taikoo Place, 979 King's Road,
Quarry Bay, Hong Kong

Oxford
Progressive
English Readers

CONTENTS

THE COMING OF THE MARTIANS

The unseen threat

No one, in the last few years of the nineteenth century, would have believed that our world was being watched closely by minds much greater than mankind's, and yet as mortal as our own. As men and women were going about ⁵ their lives they were being watched and studied, perhaps almost as closely as a human scientist might study, through a microscope, the creatures that live in a drop of water.

No one at that time gave a thought to the older worlds of space. If they did think about them at all, they never ¹⁰ imagined that the other planets could be a threat to human life. The most that people imagined was that there could possibly be some form of life on Mars, but that any creatures there would be less intelligent than ourselves, and in need of our help. ¹⁵

Yet across the miles of space, minds that made our minds seem as simple as those of animals, looked at Earth with jealous eyes. Slowly and surely they made their plans against us. And early in the twentieth century people on Earth found out how wrong they had been about Mars. ²⁰

The planet Mars goes round the sun at a distance of 140 million miles. It receives about half the light and heat from the sun that we do. It must be older than our world, and life on its surface must have begun long before our world cooled. It is smaller than Earth, and this fact must ²⁵ have hurried its cooling to the temperature at which life could begin. It has air and water, and all that is necessary for animal life.

No writer, up to the very end of the nineteenth century, expressed any idea that intelligent life might have ³⁰ developed there. But Mars is an older planet than our Earth and further away from the sun. Life on it must therefore be older, and more advanced, than life on our world. Not many people understood this then.

5 The long cooling that must some day happen to our planet had already gone far with our neighbour in space. We now know that even in its warmest parts the midday temperature is colder than our coldest winter. Its air is much thinner than ours, its oceans are now so small that 10 they cover only a third of its surface.

During the last hundred years, some of the Martians realized that if they stayed on their old, dying planet, they themselves would die out. They must therefore move to a new home. And looking across space, with instruments 15 and knowledge such as we have scarcely dreamt of, they saw our own warm planet. At its nearest distance it is only 35 million miles away from them. They could see that it was green with all kinds of plants and blue with water. Through the clouds they saw broad areas of populated 20 country and narrow blue seas.

And we humans, the creatures who inhabit this world, must have seemed to them as different and simple as monkeys seem to us.

Life, for mankind, is a continual struggle for existence, 25 and it would seem that it was also a struggle on Mars. Their world had gone far in its cooling, and our world seemed crowded with life. But crowded only with what the Martians thought of as animals. To escape from the slow destruction that year after year crept up on them, 30 their only hope was to move to a new home; one that was closer to the sun.

The Martians seem to have calculated their journey through space with amazing cleverness, and to have prepared everything perfectly. They took time, making 35 sure that everything would go well. If our telescopes had been better, we might have seen the gathering trouble far back in the nineteenth century.

Bright lights on Mars

It all began six years ago. Lavelle, a scientist working in Java, reported the sudden appearance of a very bright light upon the planet Mars. It had happened towards midnight on the twelfth of August. His scientific instruments showed that the light was caused by an explosion of flaming gas, mainly hydrogen, which seemed to be moving very fast, and straight towards the Earth. This stream of fire disappeared at about a quarter past twelve. He compared it to a huge cloud of flame suddenly and violently shot out of the planet, 'as flaming gas rushes out of a gun'.

This proved to be an extremely accurate description. Yet the next day there was only a little note in one newspaper, the *Daily Telegraph*, about it. The world still knew nothing of the greatest danger that ever threatened the human race.

I might not have heard of the flaming gas at all, but then I met Ogilvy, the well-known astronomer, at Ottershaw, a small town near my home. He was very excited at the news, and asked me if I would like to take turns with him watching the red planet through his telescope.

In spite of all that has happened since, I still remember that night very clearly. As I looked through the telescope, I saw a circle of deep blue. In the centre of the circle was the planet Mars. It seemed such a little thing, so bright and small and still. It was 40 million miles away from us.

And invisible to me, because it was much too small to see at that distance, flying steadily towards Earth across the emptiness of space, drawing nearer and nearer every minute, came the Thing they were sending us. The Thing that was to bring so much suffering to the Earth. I never dreamt of it then as I watched; not one person on Earth dreamt of that well-aimed missile.

That night, too, there was another shooting out of bright, hot gas from the distant planet. I saw a reddish flash on the outline of the planet, just as the clock struck midnight. I told Ogilvy and he took my place. He got very excited, watching the stream of gas that came towards us.

That night another invisible missile started on its way to the Earth from Mars, just twenty-four hours after the first one. Ogilvy watched until one o'clock, and then gave up. We lit a lamp and walked from the observatory to his house. Down below us in the darkness were the little towns of Ottershaw and Chertsey, with all their hundreds of people, sleeping in peace.

Many other observers saw the flame that night. They saw another the night after, also about midnight, and again the night after that, and so on for ten nights, a flame each night. The daily papers began printing stories about the fires on Mars. And, without anyone knowing, those missiles the Martians had fired came ever closer. They were travelling at many miles a second through space, hour by hour, day by day, nearer and nearer.

One night I went for a walk with my wife around Maybury, the village where we lived. The sky was full of stars. We looked at the planet Mars, a bright dot of light, towards which so many telescopes were pointed. It was a warm night. As we walked home, a group of holiday-makers passed us from Chertsey or Isleworth after a day out on the River Thames. They were singing and playing music. There were lights on in the upper windows of many of the houses as people went to bed.

From the railway station in the distance came the sound of trains. It all seemed so safe and calm.

The falling star

Months later, in June the following year, came the first of the falling stars. It was seen late one Thursday night, a line of flame, high in the sky. Hundreds of people must have seen it, and thought that it was just an ordinary falling star.

I was at home at that hour and writing in my room. The curtains were drawn back, for I love to look at the night sky, but I didn't see the falling star. It must have passed over while I was sitting there and, if I had looked up, I should have seen it. Some people said it fell with a hissing sound, and most of them thought it was a large meteorite. No one bothered to look for the fallen mass that night.

But very early on the Friday morning, Ogilvy, who had seen the shooting star, went out to find it. He was sure that the meteorite lay somewhere on the common, the open grassland that lies between the towns of Horsell, Ottershaw and Woking. He found it soon after dawn, not far from the sand pits. It had made a huge hole in the ground where it fell, and the sand and stones had been thrown violently in all directions. There were large heaps of sand which could be seen from a mile and a half away. The grass all around was on fire, and thin blue smoke rose into the air.

The Thing itself lay almost completely buried in sand. The uncovered part looked like a huge cylinder. It had a diameter of about thirty yards. Ogilvy went nearer. He was surprised by its size, and even more surprised by its shape,
5   for most meteorites are almost completely round. It was, however, still hot from its flight, and he could not go too close to it. He heard a slight noise coming from the cylinder, and thought that it was the surface of the Thing cooling. He never dreamed, at that time, that it might be
10 hollow.

He stood at the edge of the pit it had made for itself, staring at its strange appearance. It had a most unusual shape and colour. The early morning was very still, and the sun, just rising over the trees towards Weybridge, was
15 already warm. He did not remember hearing any birds singing that morning, there was no wind, and the only sounds came from the cylinder. He was all alone on the common.

Then suddenly he noticed that some grey ash, which
20 covered the top of the cylinder, was falling off. A large piece suddenly came off and fell with a sharp noise that startled him.

For a minute he did not realize what this meant. Although it was very hot, he climbed down into the pit
25 to see the Thing more clearly. What could be making the ash drop off like that?

The turning of the screw

And then he saw that the circular top of the cylinder was turning. It was such a gradual movement that he
30 discovered it only from observing a black mark on the side of the Thing. Five minutes before, the mark had been near him, and now it was over on the far side, away from him. He still did not realize what was happening, until he heard a scraping sound and saw the black
35 mark move forward an inch or so. Then he understood.

The cylinder was hollow — with an end that screwed out! Something inside was unscrewing the top!

'Good heavens!' said Ogilvy. 'There's a man in it — men in it! Half burned to death! Trying to escape!'

It was then, for the first time, that he connected the Thing with the flashes on Mars.

The thought of the poor creatures inside was so dreadful to him that he forgot the heat, and went forward to the cylinder to try to help turn the top. But luckily the heat stopped him before he could burn his hands on the still glowing metal. He stood still for a minute, uncertain what to do. Then he turned, climbed quickly out of the pit, and set off running wildly into Woking. The time must have been about six o'clock in the morning. He raced along the road until he saw Henderson, a London author, at work in his garden. He called to him over the fence.

'Henderson,' he called, 'Did you see that shooting star last night?'

'Yes, what about it?' said Henderson.

'It's out on Horsell Common now.'

'Good Lord!' said Henderson. 'A fallen meteorite! That's good.'

'No! Not a meteorite. Something much more interesting than that! It's a metal cylinder — a man-made cylinder! And there's something inside it.'

Henderson stopped what he was doing and stood up with his spade in his hand.

'What's that?' he said. He was deaf in one ear, and wondered if he had heard correctly.

Ogilvy told him all that he had seen. Henderson dropped his spade, picked up his jacket, and came out to the road. The two men hurried back to the common, and found the cylinder still lying in the same position. But now the sounds inside had stopped. A thin, bright circle of metal showed between the top and the body of the cylinder. Air was either entering or escaping at the edge with a soft hissing sound.

They listened, and banged on the side of the Thing with a stick, but there was no reply. They decided that the man or men inside must be unconscious, or dead.

Of course the two were quite unable to do anything. They shouted that they would bring help, and went off back to Woking again. One can imagine them, covered with sand, excitedly running up the main street in the bright sunlight. The town was just beginning to wake up. Henderson went into the railway station at once to send a message to London.

By eight o'clock a number of people had already started for the common to see the 'dead men from Mars'. That was the story that was told. I heard of it first from my newspaper-boy, at about a quarter to nine, when I went to get my morning paper. I was naturally very surprised, and lost no time in going out to the sand pits on the common.

THE FIRST DEATHS

On Horsell Common

I found a little crowd of perhaps twenty people surrounding the huge hole in which the cylinder lay. Henderson and Ogilvy were not there. I think they realized that nothing could be done for the present, and had gone away to have breakfast.

There were four or five boys sitting on the edge of the pit. They were having great fun, throwing stones at the giant Thing. I stopped them and they went to play somewhere else. There was very little talking among the crowd. Few of the common people in England at that time knew anything about astronomy. Most of them were staring quietly at the big table-like end of the cylinder, which was still as Ogilvy and Henderson had left it. Some went away while I was there, and other people came. I went down into the pit and was sure I felt a faint movement under my feet. The top had certainly stopped turning.

At that time I was quite sure in my own mind that the Thing had come from the planet Mars. I thought, however, that it was unlikely that it contained any living creatures. I did believe that there were intelligent beings on Mars, but not that they would come to visit us. Perhaps they had sent this Thing with messages for us. There might be some writing inside, which would take years to understand. Or perhaps there were coins and models in it. Yet it was surely too big for that purpose. I was impatient to see it opened. About eleven o'clock, as nothing seemed to be happening, I walked back to my house in Maybury. But I found it difficult to work at my writing.

In the afternoon there were far more people on the common. The early evening papers had surprised London with enormous headlines:

'A MESSAGE RECEIVED FROM MARS'
'Amazing Story from Woking'

and so on. Also, Ogilvy had excited every observatory in the country by telling them about the Thing.

The weather was extremely hot. There was not a cloud in the sky, nor a breath of wind. The grass fire had been put out, but the level ground towards Ottershaw was black as far as one could see.

Going to the edge of the pit, I found a group of about half a dozen men down in it. Henderson and Ogilvy were there, and a tall man with fair hair. I afterwards learnt that he was Stent, the famous astronomer. There were also several workmen with spades. Stent was giving directions. He was standing on the cylinder, which was now, it seems, rather cooler. However, his face was bright red with the heat, and the work.

A large part of the cylinder had been uncovered, though its lower end was still sunk deep into the ground. As soon as Ogilvy saw me among the staring crowd on the edge of the pit, he called to me to come down. He asked me if I would mind going over to see Lord Hilton, who lived in the big house on the edge of the common.

The growing crowd, he said, was beginning to be an annoyance, especially the boys. They wanted a fence put up, to help to keep the people back. He told me that faint noises could still be heard coming from the cylinder, but that the workmen had failed to unscrew the top. There was nothing for them to hold, in order to turn it.

I was very glad to do as he asked. Lord Hilton was not at home, but I was told that he was expected from London by the six o'clock train. As it was then about a quarter past five, I went home, had some tea, and walked up to the station to meet him.

The cylinder opens

It was sunset when I returned to the common. The crowd about the pit had grown larger, and stood out black against the lemon-yellow of the evening sky. There must have been about two hundred people there.

The end of the cylinder was again being unscrewed from inside. Somebody knocked into me, and I narrowly missed being thrown down into the pit. I turned, and as I did so the top must have come off. The lid of the cylinder fell with a great ringing sound. I turned my head towards the Thing again.

For a moment that circular hole seemed perfectly black. I had the sunset in my eyes.

I think everyone expected to see a man come out — possibly something a little unlike earthly men, but a man all the same. I know I did. But, looking, I presently saw something moving in the shadow — greyish, swelling movements, one above the other, and then two glowing circles like eyes. Then something like a little grey snake, about as thick as a walking-stick, twisted up out of the middle, and came through the air towards me — and then another.

I felt suddenly very cold with fear. There was a loud scream from a woman behind. I half turned, keeping my eyes fixed upon the cylinder. Other snake-like tentacles were now showing over the top of the cylinder and I
5 began pushing my way back from the edge of the pit. The people around me were horrified. I heard shouts on all sides. There was a general movement backward. I found myself alone, and saw the people on the other side of the pit running off. I looked again at the cylinder, and a
10 violent terror held me still. I stood and stared in horror.

A big greyish mass, the size, perhaps, of a large bear, was rising slowly and painfully out of the cylinder. As it swelled up and caught the light, its skin gleamed like the thick wet skin of an enormous fish, just pulled from the
15 water. Two large dark-coloured eyes looked at me steadily. Its head was rounded, and had, one might say, a face. There was a mouth under the eyes, which trembled and breathed heavily, and was dripping wet.

Those who have never seen a living Martian can
20 scarcely imagine the strange horror of their appearance. The peculiar V-shaped mouth with its pointed upper lip; the absence of a chin beneath the lower lip; the continual trembling of this mouth; the groups of tentacles around it; the heavy breathing in the strange air of this world; the
25 slow, painful way the creatures move about; and, above all, those huge staring eyes. I felt sick. There was something about their damp grey skin, something in their clumsy movements, that was so dreadful I cannot describe it. Even at this first sight I was terrified.

30 Suddenly the monster disappeared. It had fallen over the top edge of the cylinder into the pit. I heard it give a peculiar cry, and then another of these creatures appeared at the opening of the cylinder.

At that, I turned and ran madly towards the first group
35 of trees, perhaps a hundred yards away. But I ran sideways, almost falling, for I could not turn my face away from these horrible things.

The heat-ray

The sight of the Martians coming out of their cylinder made me so frightened that, when I reached the shelter of the trees, I stood there, unable to move further away. I stared at the heap of sand that hid them from my sight. I was full of fear and curiosity.

I did not dare to go back towards the pit, but I felt I must somehow see what was happening there. So I began to walk in a big curve, looking for a high place that would give me a view over the sand heaps into the pit. Once a group of thin black whips, like the arms of an octopus, flashed up into the air. Afterwards a thin rod rose up, joint by joint, on top of which was a circular mirror which turned about with an unsteady movement. What could be going on there?

It was nearly dark before anything else happened. The crowd far away on the left, towards Woking, seemed to grow. The little group of people towards Chobham went away. There was scarcely any movement from the pit.

It was this, as much as anything else, that gave people courage. As the evening grew darker, a slow movement towards the sand pits began. People began to move forward in twos and threes. They would advance, stop, watch, and advance again. I, too, on my side of the pit, began to move towards it.

At about half-past eight I noticed a little group of men. They were about thirty yards from the pit, coming from the direction of Horsell. A man in front of the group was waving a white flag. They moved slowly, nearer and nearer the pit.

This was the Deputation. It seems there had been a hasty meeting. The Martians were evidently intelligent creatures, in spite of their awful appearance. It had been decided to show them by signals that we, too, were intelligent.

The flag waved, first to the right, then to the left. The Deputation was too far away for me to recognize anyone, but I found

5 out afterwards that Ogilvy, Stent and Henderson were among them. A number of dim black figures followed this group at a safe distance.

Suddenly there was a flash of light, and a quantity of glowing greenish smoke came out of the pit in three clear

10 clouds. This smoke was very bright. At the same time a faint hissing sound could be heard.

The little group of people with the white flag stood still, watching and listening. As the green smoke rose, their faces flashed out pale green, and faded again as it

15 disappeared.

Then the hissing changed to humming. Slowly a metal box-shaped object rose out of the pit, and a beam of light seemed to flash out from it.

Suddenly, from the little group of men came flashes of

20 flame, a bright line of lights leaping from one to another. It was as if some invisible fire touched them and flashed into white flame. It was as if each man was suddenly at that moment turned into fire.

Then, by the light of these flames, I saw them falling,

25 and the people behind them turning and running.

I stood staring, not yet realizing that this was death leaping from man to man in that distant little crowd. All I felt was that it was something strange. There was another almost noiseless, blinding flash, and a man burst into flame, fell on his face and lay still. And as the unseen beam of heat passed over them, trees burst into flames. Far away I saw the flashes of trees and hedges and wooden buildings suddenly set on fire.

It was sweeping round quickly and steadily, this invisible sword of heat. I saw it coming towards me by the flashing bushes it touched, and was too surprised to move. It was as if an invisible red-hot finger was drawn through the grass between me and the Martians. All along a curving line beyond the sand pits the dark ground smoked and burned. Something fell with a crash, far away to the left where the road from Woking joins the common. Suddenly the humming stopped, and the black, box-like object sank slowly out of sight into the pit.

All this happened so quickly that I had stood through all of it without moving, blinded by the flashes of light. I was very lucky to have been outside the circle which the invisible beam cut for itself.

The common seemed now very dark, and suddenly empty of people. Overhead the stars were appearing, and in the west the sky was still a pale, bright, almost greenish, blue. The Martians and their cylinder were altogether invisible, except for that thin rod, upon which their restless mirror moved. Patches of grass and one or two trees smoked and glowed, and some houses on the road leading to Woking were on fire.

The little group of black figures with the white flag had been swept out of existence. I realized with a shock that I was helpless and alone on the dark common. Suddenly I knew that I was afraid.

With an effort I turned and began to run away through the long grass.

3

SOLDIERS AND GUNS

Panic in the Chobham Road

It is still a mystery how the Martians make this ray which kills people so quickly and so silently. Anything that can burn flashes into flame at its touch. It melts lead and makes it run like water, it softens iron, cracks and melts glass, and when it falls on water there is a great explosion of steam.

That night, nearly forty bodies lay under the stars, round the pit, burned beyond recognition. And all night long the common from Horsell to Maybury was burning brightly.

The dreadful news probably reached Chobham, Woking and Ottershaw at about the same time.

Earlier that evening, after the shops closed, the shop-people and their friends had all made their way to the common to see what was happening. At that time, only a few people in Woking even knew that the cylinder had opened, though poor Henderson had sent a messenger on a bicycle to the post office with a special message to an evening paper.

As these people came out, by twos and threes, to the common, they found little groups of people talking excitedly, and looking at the spinning mirror over the sand pits.

By half-past eight, when the Deputation was destroyed, there may have been a crowd of about three hundred people or more at this place on the edge of the common, by the Chobham Road. There were other people, too, who had left the road to go nearer to the Martians. Three policemen, one of whom was on horse-back, were at the edge of the pit, doing their best, under instructions from Stent, to keep the people back.

Stent and Ogilvy had expected that there might be trouble, and they had sent a message to the army as soon as the Martians came out of the cylinder. They had no idea, then, what was about to happen. They wanted some soldiers to protect these strange creatures from the violence of the crowd. When they had sent this message from Horsell, they returned to lead the Deputation.

The description of their death, as it was seen by the crowd, is the same as mine; the three green clouds of smoke, the deep humming noise, and the flashes of flame.

But that crowd of people had a far narrower escape than me. Only the fact that a small sand-hill got in the way of the lower part of the heat-ray saved them. If the mirror had been a few yards higher in the air, none of them would have lived to tell the story. They saw the flashes, and the men falling, and an invisible hand, so it seemed, lit the bushes as it hurried towards them. Then, with a whistling noise, the beam swung over their heads, lighting the tops of the trees that lined the road. It touched a small group of houses, smashing bricks, shattering windows and bringing down in ruins a part of one house.

Burning leaves began to fall into the road. Hats and dresses caught fire. Then came the noise of cries from around the sand-pit. There were screams and shouts, and suddenly the policeman on the horse came galloping through the crowd with his hands covering his head, trying to protect himself from the ray.

'They're coming!' a woman screamed, and at once everyone was turning and pushing at those behind, trying to get back to Woking again. Where the road becomes narrower the crowd got stuck, and in the panic there was
5 a desperate struggle. Not all of that crowd escaped; three persons at least, two women and a little boy, were knocked down and trodden on and left to die in the darkness.

The circle of excitement

10 On that Friday night, if you had drawn a circle of five miles around the Horsell Common sand-pits, I doubt if you would have had one human being outside it who was in any way affected by these new arrivals from Mars. By then, many people had heard of the cylinder, of course,
15 but it did not mean much to them.

Even within the circle, most people were not affected. All over the district, life was going on as normal. People were eating and drinking; men were gardening after their day's work; mothers were putting children to bed; young
20 people were wandering through the lanes; students sat reading their books.

Maybe there was talking in the village streets, and here and there a messenger, or even an eye-witness, telling people about the later happenings, which caused
25 excitement and shouting. But for most people the daily business of working, eating, drinking and sleeping went on as it had done for hundreds of years. It was as though no planet Mars existed in the sky. Even at Woking and Horsell and Chobham it was the same.

30 In Woking station, until very late, trains were stopping and going on. Passengers were getting out and waiting, and everything was completely normal. A boy from the town was selling newspapers containing the afternoon's news.

'Men from Mars!' he was shouting.

A group of people came into the station at about nine o'clock, very excited with the unbelievable news. They caused no more disturbance than fools might have done. People rattling towards London looked out of the windows of the train into the darkness, and saw the occasional flash of flame. They all thought it was nothing more serious than a grass fire caused by lightning. It was only round the edge of the common that any unusual disturbance was noticeable. There, half a dozen houses were burning. All night long, lights were on in the houses of the three villages at the sides of the common — Horsell, Chobham and Ottershaw — and people stayed awake till dawn.

Later that night a curious crowd gathered, both on the Chobham and Horsell roads. One or two adventurous people, it was afterwards found, went into the darkness and crawled quite near to the Martians; but they never returned. For now and again a light-ray, like the beam of a warship's light, searched the common, and the heat-ray was ready to follow. Except for that, the big area of common was silent and empty, and the burned bodies lay on it all night under the stars, and all the next day. Many people said they could hear the noise of hammering coming from the pit that night.

This was the state of things on that Friday night. In the centre, sticking into the skin of our planet Earth like a poisoned arrow, was the cylinder. But the poison was hardly working yet. Around it was a patch of silent common, smoking in places, and with a few dark objects lying in peculiar positions. Here and there was a burning bush or tree. Beyond was a circle of excitement, but outside that circle, the excitement had not yet crept. In the rest of the world, life still went on as it had for many, many years. The fever of war, that would presently attack the heart of our world, had still to develop.

All night long the Martians were hammering and moving about in the pit at work on the machines they were making ready. They never seemed to get tired; they never slept. Now and again a cloud of greenish-white smoke rose up to the sky, which was bright with stars.

At about eleven o'clock that night, soldiers came through Horsell, and spread out along the edge of the common. Several officers had been on the common earlier in the day and one, Major Eden, was reported to be missing. The officer in command came to Chobham Bridge, and was busy questioning the crowd at midnight. The army certainly knew how serious this business was.

A few seconds after midnight the crowd in Chertsey Road, Woking, saw a star fall from heaven into the woods to the north-west. It fell with a greenish light, causing a flash like summer lightning. This was the second cylinder.

The fighting begins

Saturday was strangely peaceful, but we were all waiting for something to happen. I had not slept very well, and I rose early. I went into my garden before breakfast, and stood looking out towards the common, and listening, but nothing seemed to be moving out there.

The milkman came as usual. I heard the rattle of his cart, and I went round to the side gate to ask the latest news. He told me that during the night the Martians had been surrounded by soldiers, and that big guns were expected to arrive very soon.

'They say that the Martians must not be killed,' said the milkman, 'if that can possibly be avoided.'

I saw my neighbour gardening, and talked to him for a time.

'It's a pity they are so unfriendly,' he said. 'It would be interesting to know how they live on another planet. We might learn something useful.'

At the same time he told me of the burning of the woods just outside Byfleet.

'I've heard,' he said, 'that there's another of those horrible things fallen there — number two.'

The woods, he said, were still burning, and he pointed out a cloud of smoke to me. He felt sure that the army would be able to capture or destroy the Martians during the day.

Nothing happened in the morning. I tried to take a look at the common, but was stopped by the soldiers. They had set up observation posts in the church towers at Horsell and Chobham. The soldiers I spoke to didn't seem to know anything; their officers were mysterious and secretive as well as busy. I found that the people felt quite safe now that the army was there. The soldiers had made those who lived on the borders of Horsell lock up and leave their homes.

I got back to lunch about two, very tired, for the day was extremely hot. Around three o'clock a gun began to fire from Chertsey or Addlestone. I learnt that the wood into which the second cylinder had fallen was being fired at, in the hope of destroying the object before it opened.

About half-past four I went up to the railway station to get an evening paper, for the morning papers had contained only a very inaccurate description of the killing of Stent, Ogilvy, Henderson and the others in the Deputation. But there was little I didn't know. The Martians did not show an inch of themselves. They seemed busy in their pit, and there was a sound of hammering and an almost continuous stream of smoke. They were clearly getting ready for a struggle. 'Fresh attempts have been made to signal to them, but without success', was all the papers said. A soldier told me it was done by a man in a ditch with a flag on a long pole. The Martians took as much notice of this signal as we should of the noise a cow makes.

At five o'clock, a large gun arrived in Chobham for use against the first group of Martians. I must confess that the sight of all these soldiers and their guns greatly

excited me. In my imagination I became a great fighter, and I defeated the Martians in a dozen different ways. Something of my schoolboy dreams of battle and bravery came back. It hardly seemed a fair fight to me at that time.
5   The Martians seemed very helpless in that pit of theirs.

About six in the evening, as I sat having tea with my wife in the garden, talking excitedly about the battle that was threatening us, I heard the noise of the large gun firing from the common, and immediately afterwards the
10 sharper sound of rifle shots. Soon after that came a violent, rattling crash, quite close to us, that shook the ground. I went into the middle of the garden, and saw the tops of the trees round the Oriental College burst into
15 smoky red flame.

The College, and the tower of the little church beside it, slid down in ruins. Then one of our chimneys cracked as if a shot had hit it, and part of it came down, making a small heap of broken pieces on the flower-bed under my study window.

We have to leave home

My wife and I stood amazed. Then I realized that the top of Maybury Hill, where our house stood, must be near enough for the Martians' heat-ray to reach it, now that the College had been cleared out of the way.

I took hold of my wife's arm and ran with her out to the road. Then I fetched our servant, telling her that I would go upstairs myself for the box she kept asking for.

'We can't possibly stay here,' I said; and as I spoke the firing began again on the common.

'But where are we to go?' said my wife, in terror.

I thought for a moment. Then I remembered my cousins.

'Leatherhead!' I shouted, above the sudden noise.

She looked away from me down the hill. The people were coming out of their houses, amazed.

'How are we to get to Leatherhead?' she said.

'Stop here,' I ordered, 'you are safe here.' And I started off at once for the Spotted Dog, for I knew that the owner of that hotel had a horse and cart. I ran, because I could see that in a moment everyone on this side of the hill would be moving. I found the owner inside, not knowing what was going on behind his house. A man stood with his back to me, talking to him.

'I must have a pound,' the landlord was saying, 'and I've no one to drive it.'

'I'll give you two,' I said, over the stranger's shoulder.

'What for?'

'And I'll bring it back by midnight,' I said.

'What's the hurry?' said the landlord. 'I'm selling my pig.

You will give me two pounds for it and you'll bring it back by midnight? What's going on now?'

I explained hastily that I had to leave my home, and wanted his horse and cart. He agreed to let me take it. Less than a minute later I was driving away with it, down the road. When I got back to my house, I rushed in to pack a few things. Then I ran to my neighbours' door, and knocked. I had heard that they were going to London that day, and wanted to be sure that they had gone. No one answered the door. Then I ran into my house again to get my servant's box. I returned, put the box beside her in the back of the cart, and jumped up into the driver's seat beside my wife. In another moment we were clear of the smoke and the noise, and going fast down the opposite side of the hill towards Old Woking.

4

THE MECHANICAL GIANTS

The storm breaks

Leatherhead is about twelve miles from Maybury Hill. The scent of hay was in the evening air as we drove through the fields beyond Pyrford. The hedges on either side were sweet and gay with wild roses. The heavy firing that had started again while we were driving down Maybury Hill had stopped, leaving the evening very peaceful and still. We got to Leatherhead safely, at about nine o'clock. The horse had an hour's rest, while I ate some supper with my cousins and gave my wife into their care.

It was nearly eleven o'clock when I decided to return. The night was unexpectedly dark. To me, walking out of the light in my cousins' house, it seemed absolutely black, and it was as hot as the day had been. Overhead the clouds were moving fast, for a storm was coming. My wife stood in the doorway, and watched me until I jumped up into the cart. Then she turned and went in, leaving my cousins side by side to wish me luck.

I was a little sad at first because of my wife's fears, but soon my thoughts were on the Martians again. At that time I knew nothing of what had been happening during the evening. I decided to return to Maybury through Ockham, and as I drove through the town I saw in the west a blood-red glow, which slowly filled more and more of the sky. The clouds of the gathering thunderstorm met and mixed there with masses of black and red smoke.

Suddenly a green light lit up everything around me, and even showed up the distant woods. I saw that the clouds had been cut, as if by a moving thread of green fire, which suddenly lit the whole sky and then dropped into the fields to my left. It was the third falling star!

Almost at the same time came the first lightning of the storm, and the thunder burst like a rocket overhead. The horse was frightened and began to gallop.

We raced down the slope towards the foot of Maybury Hill. Once the lightning had begun, it went on and on. I have never before seen anything like it. The thunder sounded like the noise of a huge electric machine. The flashing light was blinding and confusing, and thin rain hit my face as we raced down the slope.

Walking machines

At first I could see little except the road ahead of me. Then my attention was held by something on the opposite slope of Maybury Hill. At first I thought it was the wet roof of a house, but one flash of lighting following another showed it to be moving. And then, in a flash as bright as daylight, the red bricks of the house near the top of the hill, the green tops of the trees and this peculiar object showed up clear and bright.

And this thing I saw! How can I describe it? A huge object with three long, thin legs, four or five times higher than the houses, striding over the tallest trees in long, easy steps, and smashing them aside as it went. A walking machine of glittering metal, with ropes of steel hanging from it. The noise it made sounded above the thunder. A flash of lighting, and I could see it clearly, leaning over one way with two feet in the air. Then it disappeared, and then almost instantly, with the next flash, there it was again, a hundred yards nearer.

Suddenly the trees in the wood ahead of me parted; they were trodden down and broken. A second huge machine appeared, rushing, as it seemed, straight towards me. And I was galloping to meet it! At the sight of it I felt terribly afraid. Not stopping to look again, I pulled the horse's head hard round to the right, and in another moment the cart had fallen over upon the horse.

It smashed to the ground noisily, and I was thrown sideways and fell heavily into a shallow pool of water.

I crawled out almost immediately, and sat, with my feet still in the water, under a bush. The horse lay still (his neck was broken, poor animal) and by the lightning flashes I saw the damaged cart, and the wheel still spinning slowly. In another moment the huge machine went striding past me, and moved on up the hill towards Pyrford.

Seen nearer, the thing was unbelievably strange. It was a machine made of metal, with long, glittering tentacles swinging and rattling about its strange body. As it went along, the hood on top moved around like a head looking to left and right. Behind the main body was a huge basket of white metal, and clouds of green smoke shot out from the joints of the limbs as the monster went by me.

In an instant it was gone. All this I saw, uncertainly, in
the flashes of lightning.

As it passed, the machine began a deafening howl that
drowned the thunder, 'Aloo! Aloo!' and in another minute
5 it was with its companion, half a mile away, bending over
something in a field. I have no doubt this thing in the
field was the third cylinder that they had fired at us from
Mars.

Terror in the darkness

10 For some minutes I lay there in the rain and darkness
watching, by the flashes of lightning, these huge metal
machines moving about in the distance. I was very wet,
with rain above and pool-water below. It was some time
before I struggled up the bank to a drier position. Then
15 I began to think of the danger I was in.

Not far from me was a little hut made of wood,
surrounded by a patch of potato garden. I struggled to my
feet at last and, bending low and making use of every
chance of cover, I ran towards it. I hammered on the door,
20 but I could not make the people inside hear (if there were
any people inside), and after a time I stopped. I found a
ditch and succeeded in
crawling, unseen
by these monsters,
25 into the wood
near Maybury.

Under cover of the trees I walked on, wet and trembling with cold, towards my house. It was very dark in the wood, for there was now only an occasional weak flash of lightning, and the rain, which was pouring down, made it difficult to see.

If I had fully realized the meaning of all the things I had seen I should have immediately worked my way round through Byfleet to Street Cobham, and so gone back to rejoin my wife at Leatherhead. But I was sore, weary, wet to the skin, deafened and blinded by the storm, and the only thing I could think about was to get home.

I ran through the trees, fell into a ditch and hurt my knees on a piece of wood, and finally splashed out into a lane. I say splashed, for the storm water had turned the lane into a muddy stream. There, in the darkness, a man bumped into me and nearly knocked me over.

He gave a cry of terror, jumped sideways, and rushed on before I could speak to him. I had a difficult time trying to get up the hill to my house because of all the damage done by the storm. I kept close to the fence on the left of the lane and worked my way along it.

Near the top of the hill I fell over something soft. A flash of lightning showed it to be a heap of black cloth and a pair of boots. Before I could see any more, the flash of light had passed. It was a man, I felt sure, and I stood by him, waiting for the next flash. When it came I saw that he was a big man and his head was bent under his body. He lay close to the fence and it looked as if he had been thrown violently against it.

I bent down and turned him over to feel for his heart. He was quite dead. His neck had been broken. The lightning flashed for the third time and I saw his face. It was the owner of the 'Spotted Dog', whose horse and cart I had taken.

I stepped over him and went on up the hill. Nothing was burning on the hillside, though from the common

there still came a red glow and a mass of black smoke.
The houses around me did not seem to have been
damaged. By the ruined College, another dark heap lay
in the road.

5   Down the road towards Maybury Bridge I could hear
voices and footsteps, but I did not have the courage to
shout or to go to the people there. I reached my house
at last and, once inside, I closed and locked the door. I
walked slowly to the stairs and sat down. My imagination
10   was full of those metal monsters striding over the trees
and of the dead body smashed against the fence. I sat at
the bottom of the stairs with my back to the wall,
trembling violently.

Fiery confusion

15   After a time I realized how cold and wet I was. There
were pools of water around me on the stair carpet. I got
up, went into the dining-room and had a drink. Then I
changed my clothes.

After I had done that I went upstairs to my study. I
20   stood still in the doorway. The window of my study looks
over the trees and towards the railway where it goes
across Horsell Common. We had gone in such a hurry that
this window had been left open. Through it I could see
that the thunderstorm had passed. The towers of the
25   Oriental College and the trees around it had gone. Very
far away, lit by a bright red glow, I could see the common
and the sand pits. Across the red light, huge black shapes
moved busily to and fro.

It seemed as if the whole country in that direction was
30   on fire. Every now and then, smoke from some nearer fire
passed across the window and hid the Martian shapes. I
could not see what they were doing, nor recognize the black
objects they were working over. Neither could I see the
nearer fire, though the reflections of it danced upon the wall
35   and ceiling of the study. A smell of burning was in the air.

I closed the door noiselessly and crept towards the window. Now I could see much more. I could see, in one direction, as far as the houses by Woking station. In the other direction, the burned and black woods of Byfleet came into view. There was a light down below the hill on the railway, near the bridge, and several houses along the Maybury road and the streets near the station were glowing ruins. The light on the railway puzzled me for a while; there was a black heap and a bright light, and to the right of that a row of yellow squares. Then I saw that this was a wrecked train, the front part smashed and on fire, the back half still upon the rails.

And this was the little world in which I had been living safely for years, this fiery confusion! What had happened in the past seven hours I did not know. Nor did I know, though I was beginning to guess, the connection between these amazing mechanical giants and the horrible grey things I had seen struggling out of the cylinder. I sat down in front of the window and stared at the blackened country, and especially at the three huge black things that were going to and fro in the light around the sand pits.

They seemed amazingly busy. I began to wonder what they could be. Were they intelligent machines? Or did a Martian sit inside each one to drive it?

Wiped out

I don't know how long I sat there, looking out of the window. It must have been nearly dawn, when someone came into my garden. I heard a slight scraping noise, and looked down from my window. I saw a soldier climbing over the fence. At the sight of another human being my tiredness passed, and I leant out of the window eagerly.

'Hello!' I said in a whisper.

He stopped on the top of the fence, wondering who was calling. Then he came across the grass, until he was under my window.

'Who's there?' he said, also whispering and looking up.

'Where are you going?' I asked.

'God knows.'

'Are you trying to hide?'

5   'That's it.'

'Come into the house,' I said.

I went down, unfastened the door, and let him in. Then I locked the door again. It was dark so I could not see his face. He was not wearing a hat, and his coat was

10   unbuttoned.

'What has happened?' I asked.

'Everything,' he replied. 'They wiped us out — simply wiped us out.'

He followed me into the dining room.

15   'Have a drink,' I said, giving him a glass.

He drank, then suddenly he sat down at the table, put his head on his arms, and began to cry like a little boy.

5

THE LONG WAY ROUND TO LEATHERHEAD

The soldier's story

It was a long time before the soldier could answer my questions. But, bit by bit, I managed to find out what had happened while I had been away that Saturday night.

He was the driver of a gun-carriage and had only come to Horsell at about seven o'clock on the previous evening. At that time guns were firing across the common, and it was said that the first party of Martians was crawling slowly towards the second cylinder under the cover of a metal shield. Later this shield stood up on tripod legs, and became the first of the fighting-machines I had seen.

The gun that the soldier drove had been set up near Horsell. As soon as it was ready, other soldiers began to fire it at the sand-pit. The soldier's horse trod in a rabbit-hole and fell, throwing him into a hollow in the ground. At the same moment the gun exploded behind him, the ammunition blew up, there was fire all around him, and he found himself lying under a heap of dead men and dead horses.

'Wiped out!' he said again, as if he could not believe it himself.

He had hidden for a long time, looking out across the common. Other soldiers had tried to rush at the pit, but were swept out of existence. Then the mechanical monster had risen to its feet, and had begun to walk to and fro across the common, its head-like hood turning about exactly like the head of a human being. A kind of arm carried a metal box, which flashed green smoke. And out of that box came the heat-ray.

In a few minutes there was, so far as the soldier could see, not a living thing left upon the common. Every bush and tree that was not already black was burning. The giant did not touch Woking station and its group of houses until last, but the moment the heat-ray was used, the whole town became a heap of fiery ruins. Then the thing shut off the heat-ray, and began to move towards the woods where the second cylinder lay. As it did so, another glittering monster pulled itself up out of the pit.

The second monster followed the first, and only then did the soldier dare to crawl out of his hiding-place. He managed to get into the ditch along the side of the road, and so escaped into Woking.

Since then he had been trying to get nearer to London, thinking it might be safer there. People were hiding in ditches and cellars, and many of the survivors had gone to Old Woking and Send. He had been very thirsty but had found one of the water pipes near the railway bridge smashed, and the water bubbling out over the road.

Plans to return to Leatherhead

That was the story I got from him. He had eaten no food since midday on Saturday, so I found some meat and bread in the kitchen and brought it into the room. We did not light the lamp in case we attracted the Martians.

When we had finished eating we went quietly upstairs to my study, and looked out of the open window. In one night the valley had become a valley of ashes. The ruins of burned houses and blackened trees looked terrible in the bright, clear light of dawn. Yet here and there some object had had the luck to escape — a white railway signal here, the end of a garden shed there, white and fresh among the wreckage. And shining with the growing light from the east, three of the metal giants stood by the pit. Their heads were turning as though they were looking at the destruction they had produced.

It seemed to me that the pit had become larger, and sometimes clouds of bright green smoke came up out of it and rose into the air.

As the light increased we moved away from the window and went very quietly downstairs. We agreed that it was not safe to stay in the house. My plan was to return at once to Leatherhead. I had decided to take my wife to Newhaven, and go with her out of the country. I could see that the country about London must, one day, be the scene of a desperate fight before these monsters could be destroyed.

Between us and Leatherhead, however, lay the third cylinder, with its guarding giants. If I had been on my own, I think I should have taken a chance and gone across country. But the soldier persuaded me not to go that way.

'It would not be kind to your wife,' he said, 'to make her a widow.'

So in the end I agreed to go with him through the woods as far as Weybridge. From there I would go the long way round through Esher to reach Leatherhead.

Before we left I filled a bottle with milk, and we both put packets of biscuits and meat in all our pockets. Then we crept out of the house, and ran down the road.

The houses seemed empty. In the road lay a group of three burned bodies close together, struck dead by the heat-ray. Here and there were things that people had dropped in their hurry to get away. At the corner a little cart, filled with boxes and furniture, rested on a broken wheel. A metal box for keeping money in had been hastily smashed open, and thrown under the wreckage.

Except for one small house, which was still on fire, none of the other houses had suffered very greatly. The heat-ray had burned off the chimney tops and passed. Yet, except for ourselves, there did not seem to be a living person on Maybury Hill. Most of the inhabitants had escaped, or hidden.

We went down the lane, past the body of a man in black, and into the woods at the foot of the hill. We pushed through the trees towards the railway, without meeting anyone. We talked in whispers, and looked now
5 and again over our shoulders. Once or twice we stopped to listen.

'Absolute nonsense!'

After a time we came near the road. As we did so we heard the sound of horses. Looking through the trees, we
10 could see three soldiers riding slowly towards Woking. We called to them, and they stopped while we hurried towards them. One of them was an officer.

'You are the first people I've seen coming this way this morning,' said the officer. 'What's happening?'
15 His voice and face were eager. The men behind him stared curiously. The soldier jumped down the bank into the road and stood in front of the officer.

'Gun destroyed last night, sir. Have been hiding. Trying to rejoin my section, sir. You'll come in sight of the
20 Martians, I expect, about half a mile along this road.'

'What are they like?' asked the officer.

'Giants in armour, sir. Hundred feet high. A great metal hood like a head, on three long metal legs, sir.'

The officer's face showed that he thought
25 the soldier was joking.
'What absolute
nonsense!' he said.

'You'll see, sir. They carry a kind of box, sir, that shoots fire and strikes you dead.'

'What do you mean — a gun?'

'No, sir.' And the soldier began to describe the heat-ray. Halfway through, the officer interrupted him and looked up at me. I was still standing on the bank by the side of the road.

'Did you see it?' said the officer.

'It's perfectly true,' I said.

'Well,' said the officer. 'I suppose it's my business to see it too. You'd better go along and report to Brigadier-General Marvin, and tell him all you know. He's at Weybridge. Do you know the way?'

'I do,' I said. He turned his horse to the south again.

'The Martians are half a mile away, you say?' he said.

'Yes,' I answered, and pointed over the tops of the trees to the south. He thanked me and rode on with the other two. That was the last we saw of them.

People on the move

By Byfleet station we came out of the wood, and found the country calm and peaceful in the morning sunlight. The heat-ray had not reached there. If it had not been for the emptiness of some of the houses, the movement of packing in others, and the group of soldiers standing on the railway bridge, the day would have seemed very like any other Sunday.

Several farm carts were moving along the road towards Addlestone. Through the gate of a field, we saw six huge guns, all pointing towards Woking. The soldiers stood by their guns waiting. At a safe distance were the ammunition carts. Everything was ready for the fight.

'That's good!' I said. 'They will get one fair shot, anyway.'

We continued on our way. Nearer Weybridge there were a number of men making a long bank of earth. There were more guns behind it.

'They won't be able to do much good against those Martians,' said my companion. 'They haven't seen that heat-ray yet.'

The men who were digging would stop every now and again to stare over the trees towards the south-west.

No one in Weybridge could tell us where we could find Brigadier-General Marvin. The whole place was in confusion. There were carts everywhere. The inhabitants of the place were all packing. Children ran around excitedly, enjoying this unusual way of spending a Sunday.

The soldier and I sat on the steps of the drinking-fountain to have our lunch. Soldiers were warning people to move now or to hide in their cellars as soon as the firing began. We saw, as we crossed the bridge, that a crowd of people had gathered in and a round the railway station. The platform was piled with boxes and packages. The ordinary trains had been stopped, I believe, so that soldiers and guns could be taken to Chertsey. Later, I heard that a savage struggle took place for seats in the special trains that came an hour or two afterwards.

By midday we had reached the place near Shepperton Lock where the rivers Wey and Thames join. At this point there is a ferry. On the far side of the river we could see a hotel with a lawn and, beyond the trees, the tower of Shepperton church. Across the Thames, except just where the boats landed, everything was quiet, quite different from our side.

We took the ferry across the river. Three or four soldiers stood on the lawn outside the hotel. They were staring and laughing at the passengers, without offering to help them get off.

'What's that!' cried a man in a boat, suddenly startled by a noise. 'Be quiet, you fool!' said a man to a barking dog. Then the sound came again, this time from the direction of Chertsey. The sound of a large gun firing.

Horror

The fighting had started. Almost immediately more guns, across the river to our right and hidden by the trees, began firing, one after the other. A woman screamed and men shouted. Everyone stood still. Nothing could be seen except the flat fields, and a few cows feeding quietly. Then suddenly we saw a rush of smoke far away up the river, a cloud of smoke that shot up into the air. At the same time the ground moved under our feet and a loud explosion shook the air. It smashed two or three windows in the houses near us, and left us amazed.

'Here they come!' shouted a man in a blue shirt. 'There! Do you see them? Look!'

Quickly, one after the other, one, two, three, four of the Martian machines appeared, far away over the trees, across the fields near Chertsey, striding hurriedly towards the river. Strange, hooded little figures they seemed at that distance, moving with a stiff-legged, rolling walk, but as fast as flying birds. Then, advancing directly towards us from the left, came a fifth.

The armoured bodies of the Martians glittered in the sun, growing rapidly larger as they got nearer. The last one to appear waved a huge box high in the air, and the terrible heat-ray I had seen on the Friday night shot out of it and struck the town of Chertsey.

At the sight of these terrible creatures, the crowd along the water's edge seemed to turn to stone for a moment. There was no screaming or shouting but silence as they stood there in horror. Then there was a low noise and a movement of feet — a splashing from the river. A man, too frightened to drop the bag he was carrying on his shoulder, turned round suddenly and nearly knocked me down with the corner of his load. A woman pushed at me with her hand, and rushed past me. I turned, too, but I was not too frightened to be able to think clearly. The terrible heat-ray was in my mind. I had to get under water!

THE BATTLE AT SHEPPERTON LOCK

Into the water

'Get under the water!' I shouted.

I rushed right down the gravel beach and into the water. Others did the same. The stones under my feet were muddy and slippery, and the river water was so low that I ran perhaps twenty feet, scarcely waist-deep. Then, as a Martian came near, I dived forward under the surface. The splashes of people jumping from the boats into the river sounded like thunder in my ears. People were hastily landing their boats on both sides of the river.

But the Martian machine took no notice, for the moment, of the people running this way and that. When, half-drowned, I raised my head above the water, the Martian's hood pointed at the guns that were still firing across the river and, as it advanced, it swung the box which contained the heat-ray.

In another moment it was on the bank. In a stride it was halfway across the river. The knees of its front legs bent at the far bank. In another moment it had raised itself to its full height again, close to the village of Shepperton. At once the six guns which, unknown to anyone on the right bank, had been hidden on the edge of the village, fired together. The sudden bang made my heart jump. The monster was already raising the heat-ray as the first shell exploded six yards above the hood.

I gave a cry of amazement. I forgot the other four Martian monsters, as my eyes were fixed on what was happening near me. Two other shells burst in the air near the body. The hood twisted round in time to be hit directly by the fourth shell.

A Martian dies

The shell burst right in the face of the thing. The hood swelled, flashed and was torn off in a dozen pieces of red flesh and glittering metal.

'Hit!' I shouted, halfway between a scream and a cheer.

I heard more shouts from people in the water around me. I could have leapt out of the water with excitement.

The giant monster moved clumsily, but it did not fall over. Without looking where it was going, and with the heat-ray still held high in the air, it rolled on its three

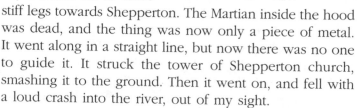

stiff legs towards Shepperton. The Martian inside the hood was dead, and the thing was now only a piece of metal. It went along in a straight line, but now there was no one to guide it. It struck the tower of Shepperton church, smashing it to the ground. Then it went on, and fell with a loud crash into the river, out of my sight. 25

A violent explosion shook the air, and water, steam, mud and pieces of metal shot far up into the sky. As the heat-ray hit the river, the water flashed into steam. In another moment a huge wave, almost boiling hot, came 30 rushing round the bend of the river towards me. I saw people struggling to get to the banks, and heard their screaming and shouting.

At this time I didn't worry about the heat. I splashed through the rough water, pushing a man aside to do so, 35 until I could see round the bend. Half a dozen empty boats rocked upon the waves. The fallen Martian came into sight, lying across the river. Most of it was under the water.

Thick clouds of steam were pouring off the wreckage. Through the steam I could see the huge metal limbs splashing about in the water and throwing mud into the air. The tentacles swayed and struck like living arms. It was as if some half-dead thing struggled for life amongst the waves. Enormous quantities of a reddish-brown liquid were shooting up noisily out of the machine. It was a horrible sight.

Suddenly my attention was taken by a man shouting to me. He was knee-deep in water, near the river bank, and was pointing. Looking behind me, I saw the other Martians coming nearer, taking huge strides down the river bank from the direction of Chertsey. The guns at Shepperton were still firing, but they did no good.

I dived under the water and, holding my breath, stayed under the surface for as long as I could. The water was rough and rapidly growing hotter.

At last I raised my head to take a breath and throw the hair and water from my eyes. The steam was rising in a white fog that hid the Martians altogether. The noise was deafening. Then I saw them dimly, huge, grey metal monsters looking even larger in the fog. They had passed by me, and two were bending over the ruins of their friend.

The third and fourth were standing beside it in the water, one perhaps two hundred yards away from me, the other towards Laleham. They waved the heat-ray boxes high in the air, and the hissing beams shot down this way and that.

The air was full of sounds, deafening and confusing: the noise of the Martians; the crash of falling houses; the sound of trees, fences and sheds flashing into flame; and the roaring of fire. Thick black smoke was leaping up to mix with the steam from the river. As the heat-rays went to and fro over Weybridge, flashes of white and smoky flames showed where they had hit.

The boiling wave

For a moment I stood there, nearly up to my neck in the almost boiling water. Through the fog I could see the people, who had been with me in the river, climbing out of the water, or running up and down on the bank in fear.

Then suddenly the white flashes of the heat-ray came leaping towards me. The houses fell apart at its touch, and burst into flames; the trees changed to fire with a roar. It flashed up and down the river bank, catching the people who ran this way and that, and came down to the water's edge, fifty yards from where I stood. It swept across the river to Shepperton, and the water in its track rose in a great boiling wave with clouds of steam pouring from the top of it. I turned towards the shore.

In another moment the huge wave, almost at boiling-point, had rushed upon me. I screamed and, half blinded and in great pain, I struggled through the leaping, hissing water towards the shore. If my foot had slipped it would have been the end. I fell helplessly, in full sight of the Martians, upon the broad, bare gravel beach. I expected death to come instantly.

I have a dim memory of the foot of a Martian coming down within twenty yards of my head. It went straight into the loose gravel, scattering it, and lifted up again. Then I remember there was a long pause, and afterwards I saw the four Martians carrying away the pieces of their friend. They became faint as they went across the fields. And then, very slowly, I realized that, by a very lucky chance, I had escaped.

The empty boat

The Martians moved back to their pit on Horsell Common. They had found out what our earthly weapons could do to them. In their hurry, carrying with them their smashed companion, they no doubt failed to capture many people like myself. If they had left their friend, and had gone on at once towards London, there was nothing, at that time, which could have stopped them.

But they were in no hurry. Every twenty-four hours another cylinder arrived from Mars, bringing more Martians to add to their number. Meanwhile the army, who now knew what it had to fight against, worked very fast. Every minute a fresh gun came into position until, before dark, every wood, every row of houses on the hilly slopes about Kingston and Richmond, hid a waiting gun.

In the area around Horsell, in the ruined villages, crawled army observers with signals to warn the soldiers that the Martians were coming. The giant machines spent the early part of the afternoon going backwards and forwards, taking everything from the second and third cylinders (the second at Addlestone, and the third at Pyrford) to their pit on Horsell Common. One huge machine was left standing over the pit to guard it. The rest of the Martians came down from their fighting-machines and went into the pit. They were hard at work there, even after dark, and the clouds of thick green smoke that rose into the air could be seen from many miles away.

While the Martians behind me were preparing for their next attack and the army in front of me was gathering for the battle, I slowly made my way from the fire and smoke towards London.

I saw an empty boat floating on the river and, throwing off most of my clothes, I dived into the water to get it.

In it I managed to escape from that scene of destruction. There were no oars in the boat, so I had to move the boat along by using my hands as paddles in the water. It took a long time, for I kept stopping and looking behind me, as you may well understand. I followed the river because I considered the water gave me the best chance of escape, if the Martians should return.

For a long time I let the river carry the boat along. I was in great pain and was very tired after the violence I had been through. Then I began to get frightened again, and hurried the boat along with my hands. The sun burned my bare back. At last, as the bridge at Walton was coming into sight round a bend, I felt so ill that I landed on the Middlesex bank. I lay down, very sick, in the long grass. I suppose the time then was about four or five o'clock. I got up presently, walked for perhaps half a mile without meeting anyone, and then lay down again in the shadow of a hedge. I seem to remember talking to myself during that walk. I was also very thirsty.

'What do these things mean?'

I must have fallen asleep for, when I opened my eyes, there was someone sitting near me. It was a churchman — a curate. He was sitting and staring up at the sky. I sat up and, at the sound of my movement, he looked at me quickly.

'Have you any water?' I asked.

He shook his head. 'You have been asking for water for the last half hour,' he said.

For a moment we looked at one another in silence. I expect he thought I was a strange-looking person. I was wearing nothing except my trousers, and my face and shoulders were blackened from the smoke. His face was fair, and his hair lay in curls on his head. His eyes were rather large, pale blue and staring. He spoke suddenly, looking directly past me.

'What does it all mean?' he said. 'What do these things mean?'

I stared at him and did not answer.

5 He held out a thin, white hand and spoke in a complaining way.

'Why are these things allowed? What
10 sins have we done to be punished in this way? I was walking through the roads to clear my brain, and then — fire, destruction, death! What are these Martians?'

'What are we?' I answered, clearing my throat.

He turned to look at me again. For half a minute,
15 perhaps, he stared silently.

'I was walking through the roads to clear my brain,' he repeated, 'and suddenly fire, destruction, death!'

He was silent again, and his chin sank to his knees.

By this time I was beginning to understand him. The
20 terrible happenings in which he had taken part — he was almost certainly from Weybridge — had made him nearly mad.

'Are we near Halliford?' I asked.

'What are we to do?' he continued. He seemed not to
25 have heard my question at all. 'Are these creatures everywhere? Has the earth been given over to them?'

I began to explain to him my ideas of what was happening. He listened for a few minutes but, as I went on, he grew less interested, and began staring again, turning his head away from me.

'This must be the beginning of the end,' he said, interrupting me. 'The end of the world! When men shall call upon the mountains and the rocks to fall on them and hide them.'

I struggled to my feet and, standing over him, laid my hand on his shoulder.

'Be a man,' I said. 'You are very frightened.'

For a time he sat in silence.

'But how can we escape?' he asked suddenly. 'We can do nothing against them.'

'The stronger they are, the more careful we must be,' I answered. 'And they can be hurt. One was killed three hours ago.'

'Killed!' he said, staring about him.

'I saw it happen,' I told him. 'We've been in the bad part of it, that's all.'

'What is that flashing light in the sky?' he asked suddenly.

I told him it was an army signal — that it was a sign that human help and effort were all around us.

'We are in the middle of the trouble,' I said, 'even though it is quiet now. The Martians are behind us, and towards London guns are being hidden to protect the city from attack. Soon the Martians will be coming this way again.'

As I spoke, he jumped to his feet, and stopped me with a wave of his hand.

'Listen!' he said.

From beyond the low hills across the water came the sound of distant guns and an unearthly crying. Then everything was still. High in the western sky the new moon hung faint and pale, above the smoke of Weybridge and Shepperton.

'We had better follow this path,' I said, 'towards the north.'

THE ADVANCE ON LONDON

London remains quiet

My younger brother was in London when the cylinders from Mars fell on the common around Woking. He was studying to be a doctor, and preparing for his final examinations. He knew nothing of the Martians until that Saturday.

Many of the morning papers on Saturday contained a very short article about them. It said that creatures in cylinders which seemed to have come from Mars had been frightened by a large crowd. They had killed a few people with a quick-firing gun. 'The Martians look quite dangerous,' said the writer at the end of his article, 'but they do not seem to be able to move out of the pit made by their cylinder. They are probably too weak from their flight through space.'

My brother was very interested in the news. From the description in the paper he worked out that the cylinders were at least two miles from our house. He knew we were not in any danger. He decided to come down to visit us on the midnight train later that night. He wanted to see the Things, he told me later, before they were all killed.

When he arrived at Waterloo railway station he heard that there had been an accident on the line. No trains were going direct to Woking. No one thought that there was anything very special about the accident, and the station staff were busy planning new routes for the Sunday trains. My brother went home, deciding to try again the following morning.

On Sunday London was still very quiet. There was more news, but most Londoners do not read the Sunday papers. Also, they are used to feeling safe. They know that surprising, frightening news can be found in the papers every day. It is nothing to get excited about.

My brother went to church in the morning, and then back to Waterloo station. He heard that no trains were running to Chertsey. A ticket collector told him that some very strange news had started coming in from Chertsey, and then it had suddenly stopped. He had been told that there was some fighting going on around Weybridge.

My brother waited at the station for some hours. During the afternoon people started coming back early from day trips into the countryside. Some people said the locks on the River Thames were closed so they could not go very far, and others thought they had heard the sound of guns firing. But no one had seen anything.

Walking back home later that afternoon my brother had to cross the river. Someone standing on Waterloo Bridge told him he had seen a dead body in the water. Two others had noticed patches of a strange brown liquid moving down the river. Someone else had seen the flashing light of an army observer's signals in the west.

Then my brother saw newspaper sellers running from Fleet Street with the latest news. 'Dreadful disaster!' they shouted as they ran. 'Fighting at Weybridge! Full description! Hundreds killed! London in danger!'

He bought a copy, and then, for the first time, he realized the awful power and terror of these monsters. He learned that they were not just weak, slow creatures trying to crawl out of their pit. They were very intelligent minds driving enormous machines. They could move surprisingly quickly. They could destroy things with such power that even the largest guns could do nothing against them. However, the newspaper article added, they could themselves be destroyed. It went on to tell of what had happened to the Martian at Shepperton Lock. There was no reason, it seemed, to think that the army had lost control. London was quite safe.

A second hit

While the curate and I sat talking under the hedge near
Halliford that Sunday evening, the Martians had started
their attack once more. I found out all this information
later, of course.

As far as one can tell from the different stories that were
told, most of the Martians had remained in the Horsell pit
until about nine that night. But three certainly came out
about eight o'clock and, spreading out and advancing
slowly and carefully, went through Byfleet and Pyrford
towards Weybridge and Ripley. These Martians did not
advance together, but in a line, each perhaps a mile and
a half from his nearest companion. They 'spoke' to each
other by means of unearthly howls, running up and down,
from one note to another. It was this howling and the
firing of the guns at Ripley and St. George's Hill that the
curate and I had heard.

The Ripley men were all part-time soldiers with no
special training. They ought never to have been placed
anywhere near the Martians. They fired their guns too
soon and all at the same time, which was useless, and
then they turned and ran away from the advancing Martian
as fast as they could go. The Martian, however, stepped
carefully among them, passed to the front of them, and
came unexpectedly to the guns in Rainshill Park, which
he destroyed.

The St. George's Hill soldiers, however, were better led,
or braver men. They were hidden by a small wood, and
seem to have been quite unexpected by the Martian
nearest to them. They fired their guns when he was about
a thousand yards away.

The shells flashed all round the Martian and they saw
him come forward a few steps, then fall down. Everybody shouted together, and the guns were reloaded in
great haste. The fallen Martian started to howl, and
immediately a second glittering giant answered him and

appeared over the trees
to the south. It looked as if
a leg of the tripod had been
smashed by one of the shells. The
gunners fired again and completely missed the Martian on
the ground. At once, both his companions pointed their
heat-rays at the battery of big guns. The ammunition blew
up, the trees all around the guns flashed into fire, and
only one or two of the men, who were already running
over the top of the hill, escaped to tell their story.   *10*

The army observers who were watching the Martians
reported that the giants remained absolutely still for the
next half-hour. The Martian who had been shot down
crawled slowly out of his hood, a small brown creature,
and repaired his tripod. At about nine o'clock he had   *15*
finished, for his fighting-machine was then seen above the
trees again.

The strange black tubes

It was a few minutes past nine that night when these three Martians were joined by four others, each carrying a thick black tube. The same sort of tube was handed to each of the other three, and the seven spread out at equal distances along a curved line between St. George's Hill, Weybridge and the village of Send, south-west of Ripley. A dozen rockets came from the observers in the hills before them as soon as they began to move, warning the gunners round Ditton and Esher. At the same time, four of the fighting-machines crossed the river. Two of them, black against the western sky, came within sight of myself and the curate, as we hurried painfully and wearily along the road that runs northward out of Halliford.

The curate cried faintly in his throat, and began running. But I knew it was no good running from a Martian. I turned and crawled through the long, wet grass into the broad ditch by the side of the road. He looked back, saw what I was doing, and came to join me.

The two Martians stopped, the one near to us standing and facing Sunbury, the other far away towards Staines.

The occasional howling of the Martians had stopped; they took up their positions in a huge half-circle round their cylinders in absolute silence. It was a half-circle with a radius of six miles, twelve miles directly from one end to the other. Never was the beginning of a battle so still.

But facing that curve everywhere, at Staines, Hounslow, Ditton, Esher, Ockham, behind hills and woods south of the river and across the flat fields to the north of it, wherever there was enough cover to hide in, the guns were waiting. The signal rockets burst bright in the night sky, and the men at the waiting guns got ready to fire their shells.

Then, after a long time, or so it seemed to us, looking through the long grass, there came a sound like the distant firing of a gun. Another nearer, and then another. And then the Martian beside us raised his tube, like a gun, and fired it. There was a loud bang that made the ground move under us. The Martian near Staines did the same. There was no flash, no smoke, simply that loud bang.

I was so excited by all this that I forgot my personal safety and burnt hands and climbed out of the ditch to stare towards Sunbury. As I did so, another bang followed, and something flew very fast over my head towards Hounslow. I expected to see smoke or fire where it landed, but there was nothing. There was no crash, no answering explosion.

'What has happened?' said the curate, standing up beside me.

'Heaven knows!' I said.

A distant shouting began and stopped. I looked at the Martian, and saw he was now moving towards the east along the river bank, with a fast, rolling movement.

Small round hills

Every moment I expected a hidden gun to fire and hit him, but none did. The Martian grew smaller as he went away and presently the darkness hid him altogether. Towards Sunbury there was something dark, as though a small round hill had suddenly grown there, hiding our view. And then across the river, over Walton, we saw another little hill. These hill-like things grew lower and broader as we watched.

I had a sudden thought, and looked northward, and there I saw a third of the cloudy black hills.

Everything had suddenly become very still. Far away to the south-east we heard the Martians howling to one another, and then the air shook again with the distant noise of their guns. But our gunners did not reply.

At the time, we could not understand these things; but later I found out the meaning of these peculiar hills. Each of the Martians, standing in the great half-circle I have

described, had used his tube to shoot out a huge metal drum. These drums were fired at any wood, house or hill where the Martian thought guns could be hidden. Some fired only one of these, some two. The one at Ripley is
5 said to have fired at least five.

These drums smashed on striking the ground — they did not explode — and they let out an enormous quantity of thick black mist, curling and pouring upwards in a huge, awful cloud, a hill of gas that sank and spread itself
10 slowly over the surrounding countryside. To breathe in that black mist was certain death.

Then the fourth cylinder fell in Bushey Park. The guns on the Richmond and Kingston line of hills began to fire, and there was a noise of shooting far away in the south-
15 west. I believe these guns must have been fired just before the black mist came down over the gunners.

The Martians spread this strange, deadly mist over the countryside near London. The ends of the half-circle slowly spread apart, until at last they formed a line from
20 Hanwell to Coombe and Malden. All night their destructive tubes advanced. Never once, after the Martian at St. George's Hill was hit, did they give the guns the slightest chance against them. If there was the least possibility that guns were hidden and waiting for them, a fresh drum of
25 the black mist was shot from their tubes. Where the guns could be seen they used the heat-ray.

The Martians did not use the heat-ray machines very much that night. Perhaps they only had a little of the material which was needed to make them work. Or
30 perhaps they didn't want to destroy the country but only to show the population how strong they were, and make them afraid. If this was their aim, they certainly succeeded. After Sunday night no attempt was made to organize guns and men against them. No group of men had any chance,
35 even with the largest guns. It was all so hopeless.

We can only imagine what must have happened to the guns and the men who worked them around Esher, for

there were no survivors. We may picture the gunners
waiting by their guns, the ammunition close by, the horses
and carts all around, the groups of village and town
people standing as near as they were
allowed. Then the bang from the
Martian tube, and the clumsy
drum flying over their
heads, and smashing
in the neighbouring
fields.

We may picture, too, the sudden loss of
interest in the guns, the turning of eyes towards the fast-
spreading curls of black mist which darkened the evening
sky. Everyone looked at this strange and horrible black
mist, coming down upon the men, women, children and   15
animals, and killing them all within seconds. There must
have been a lot of screaming and shouting as people and
horses ran in all directions to try to escape. And then
nothing: only a silent mass of blackness hiding its dead.

Before dawn the black mist was pouring through the   20
streets of Richmond. And then, at last, the people of
London realized that to save their lives they must get
away.

THE *THUNDER* CHILD

Moving away from London

Fear spread quickly through the streets of London early on Monday morning. Everyone in the city was trying to get away as fast as possible, before the arrival of the
5 Martians. There were great crowds of people at all the railway stations from which trains left for the north and east of England. There were too many for the police, who could not control the frightened population. People fought savagely for standing room in the trains, and many were
10 badly hurt, because guns and knives were used.

Later in the day the men driving the trains refused to go back to London, so other means of escape had to be found. At midday a Martian was seen at Barnes, and a cloud of black mist came along the Thames and stopped
15 all hope of escaping over the bridges across the river. The black clouds were everywhere.

If one had been in a balloon hanging over London on that June morning, one would have seen confusion everywhere. All the roads leading away from the great city
20 were crowded with people trying to escape. Never before had so many people moved and suffered together.

Directly below, one would have seen the streets, houses, churches, squares and gardens already abandoned, spread out like a great map. Over Ealing,
25 Richmond and Wimbledon, it would also have seemed as if a huge pen had dropped ink upon the map. Steadily, continuously, each black splash grew and spread, shooting out this way and that exactly as ink would spread if it were spilt on cloth.

30 And beyond, over the blue hills that rise to the south of the river, the glittering Martians went to and fro,

spreading their poison-clouds and taking control of the country for themselves. They exploded any stores of ammunition they came to, cut every telephone wire, and wrecked the railways here and there. They were putting mankind out of action.

They did not come beyond the central part of London all that day, and it is possible that a great number of people in London stayed in their houses through Monday morning. It is certain that many died at home, helpless against the black mist.

I shall presently be telling you in detail about the fifth cylinder. So it is enough, now, to say that it fell. The sixth fell at Wimbledon.

It was not long before the crowds escaping from London began to realize that they needed food. They were so hungry that they did not care how they got it. Farmers went out to guard their cattle sheds, grain stores and crops with guns in their hands. A number of people became so desperate that they even went back towards London to get food. The Government moved from London to Birmingham, where enormous quantities of ammunition were prepared.

By Tuesday a few trains began to run again. There was a notice in Chipping Ongar which said that there were large stores of flour in the northern towns and that, within twenty-four hours, bread would be given to the starving people in the neighbourhood. That night the seventh cylinder fell upon Primrose Hill.

On the Essex coast

My brother, very luckily for him, managed to get out of London on the Monday. He made his way east to Chelmsford, in Essex. At first he thought he would stay there, but on Tuesday morning he decided to push on to the coast. He hoped that he would be able to find a ship that would take him out of the country. By midday he reached Tillingham. The streets and houses there were strangely silent and empty. Past Tillingham he suddenly came in sight of the sea, and the most amazing crowd of boats and ships that it is possible to imagine.

5   Because of the black mist, sailors had found they could no longer come up the Thames, so they sailed to the Essex coast, to Harwich and The Naze and Clacton, and afterwards to Foulness and Shoebury. They, of course, had heard about the Martians, and came to take people away

10   from the fighting. The ships and boats lay in a huge curve that disappeared into the distance towards The Naze.

15   Close to the Essex shore, my brother saw hundreds of fishing boats, English, Scotch, French, Dutch, Danish, Norwegian and Swedish. Fishermen from all the countries around the North Sea had come to help. There were also boats from the Thames, small sailing boats, steam-boats

20   and electric boats, that never usually left the river. Beyond them were larger ships, coal carriers covered in dust, smart, clean merchant ships, cattle-ships, ferries, oil tankers, and an old white army transport ship. Further out beyond them were neat white and grey ocean-going

25   passenger liners from Southampton and Hamburg. All along the coast on the far side of the River Blackwater, my brother could see a great crowd of little boats taking people from the beaches, and another crowd of the same kind going right along the river, almost as far as Maldon.

About two miles out at sea was one of the strange new warships called a torpedo-ram. It was lying very low in the water. It looked, my brother thought, almost as if it were full of water, and about to sink. This was the *Thunder Child*. Torpedo-rams have powerful guns, but 5 unlike most other warships, they use their great speed and enormous strength to attack enemy ships by crashing into them.

The *Thunder Child* was the only warship in sight, but far away, to the west, over the calm, flat sea, rose parallel 10 lines of black smoke showing where the other ships of the English Fleet were. They were waiting in a long semi-circle across the mouth of the River Thames. They had already been there for three days, watchful and ready for action, but powerless to stop the Martian attack. 15

The Martians again

My brother got down onto the beach and called to some men on a paddle-steamer from the Thames. They sent a rowing boat across. They said the steamer was going to Ostend and would take him for twelve pounds. He bought 20 a ticket, and got into the boat.

It was about two o'clock when my brother finally found himself safely aboard. There was food on sale, but at very high prices. He bought some bread and cheese, and a bottle of wine, and found a seat at the front of the 25 steamer. He sat there enjoying his first meal in more than two days.

There were already about forty people on board, but the captain waited until five in the afternoon, picking up more and more passengers. The steamer became 30 dangerously crowded. The captain would probably have stayed longer but at about that time the sound of guns could be heard coming from the south. As if in answer, the torpedo-ram fired a small gun and a string of flags was raised. Smoke flew upwards out of her funnels. 35

Some of the passengers thought that the firing came from Shoebury, until it was noticed that it was growing louder. At the same time, far away in the south-east, the upper parts of three large war ships appeared one after the other, far in the distance, beneath clouds of black smoke.

The paddle-steamer was already moving east towards the big line of ships, and the low Essex coast was growing smaller, when a Martian appeared. He looked quite tiny and harmless, because he was so far away. He was advancing along the muddy coast from the direction of Foulness. When the captain of the paddle-steamer saw the Martian he shouted with fear and anger. The paddles of the steamer seemed to catch his terror, and started turning quickly. Every person aboard stood at the side or up on the seats of the steamer and stared at the distant shape. It was higher than the trees or church towers, and advancing slowly.

It was the first Martian my brother had seen. He stood, more amazed than terrified, watching the giant machine moving towards the ships. When the Martian reached the shore he did not stop, as everyone had expected. He went straight into the water, and kept on walking.

Then, farther to the south, came another Martian, stepping over some small trees, and then yet another, still farther off, moving slowly across a shiny mud-flat. They were all going towards the sea. It seemed as if they planned to stop the hundreds of ships, crowded together between Foulness and the Naze, from escaping.

In the little paddle-steamer the engines were running harder than they had ever run before. The paddles were turning faster and faster, throwing great amounts of white water up into the air. But the steamer moved away from these awful Martians with terrifying slowness.

Looking north, my brother saw the long line of ships already on the move because of the approaching terror; one ship passing behind another, others trying to turn

and getting in the way of the rest, ships whistling and
hooting, and shooting great clouds of steam into the air,
sails being let out, and smaller boats rushing backwards
and forwards between the larger ones. His attention was
so fixed on this and on the danger moving ever nearer   5
from the west that he had no time to think about anything
else. Then suddenly the steamer turned hard, and my
brother was thrown down from the seat upon which he
was standing. Everyone about him started shouting, and
running to the other side of the boat. They cheered, and   10
the cheer seemed to be answered faintly by another. He
tried to get up, but the steamer moved suddenly again
and once more he fell to the deck.

The *Thunder Child* attacks

He pulled himself up onto his feet and looked to the right.   15
There, less than a hundred yards away, he saw an
enormous iron shape like a great knife rushing through
the water. It was throwing the sea to either side in huge
white waves. These waves crashed into the little steamer,
throwing her paddles helplessly into the air, and then   20
sucking her down so that she almost went below the
water.

The iron monster passed them and was rushing towards
the land. From the two funnels came clouds of black smoke
with bright flames lighting them from inside. The torpedo-   25
ram *Thunder Child* was steaming ahead at full speed. It
was going to save the other ships from the Martians.

The steamer was moving up and down so violently that
my brother had to hold on to the side to keep himself
from falling. He looked past the *Thunder Child* to the   30
Martians again. The three of them were now close together
and had gone so far into the water that their legs were
almost completely covered. Down in the water, and at that
distance, they looked far less dangerous than the huge
iron mass that had just rushed past the paddle-steamer.   35

It would seem the Martians were observing this new enemy with some surprise. To their minds, perhaps, the giant war ship looked like another Martian. The *Thunder Child* fired no gun, but just rushed towards them at full speed. It was probably because she did not fire that she was able to get so near to them. They were not sure what she was. One shot, and they would have known, and then they would have destroyed her immediately with the heat-ray.

She was moving so fast that in a minute she seemed to be half-way between the paddle-steamer and the Martians. Suddenly, the nearest Martian pointed his tube, and shot a drum at the war ship. It hit her on the side and bounced off. The poisonous black mist that burst out when the drum hit the sea blew away harmlessly over the water. Every second the warship moved further and further away from it. A minute later, to the watchers from the steamer, with the sun in their eyes and unable to see clearly, it seemed as though she must already be among the Martians.

Suddenly there was a lot of movement. The long-legged monsters rose up out of the water and quickly moved apart as they turned back towards the shore. One of them raised his heat-ray box. He held it high, pointed it downwards towards the war ship, and the heat-ray flashed out. Super-heated steam sprang from the water it touched. It must have driven through the ship's side as easily as a white-hot iron rod through paper.

A bright flame went up through the rising steam. Then the Martian leant to one side and fell backwards. In another moment he was cut down, and a great body of water and steam shot high into the air. The guns of the *Thunder Child* sounded, going off one after the other. One shot bounced on the water close by the paddle-steamer. It then flew across the sea to the north, and smashed into a large fishing boat, turning it to match-wood.

But no one cared about that very much. When the captain of the paddle-steamer saw the Martian go down, he shouted with joy. No one could tell what he said, but no one was listening to him anyway. All the passengers crowded at the back of the steamer shouted together, too. And then they shouted again. For something long and black, with flames and smoke pouring from its middle parts, came rushing out of the great cloud of steam and water.

She was still alive! She was still under control. Her engines were still working, and she was running straight for the second Martian.

The *Thunder Child* was less than a hundred yards away from the second Martian when he used his heat-ray. Then, with a terrifying thud, and a blinding flash, her decks and her funnels leaped upward. The Martian moved back, away from the violence of the explosion, but he was too close to save himself. In another moment the mass of flaming iron, which was still driving forward very fast, hit him and smashed him down like a thing made of paper. My brother shouted with excitement. Then a boiling mass of steam, water, fire, and metal hid everything.

'Two!' yelled the captain.

Everyone was shouting. The whole steamer rang from end to end with cheers. More cheering could be heard coming from another ship, then from another, and then from all amongst the crowds of ships and boats that were sailing out to sea.

THE FIFTH CYLINDER

Trapped by the black mist

While all these things were happening in and around
London, the curate and I had been hiding in an empty
house at Halliford, where we went to escape from the
black mist. We stopped in that house all Sunday night and
all the next day, surrounded by the hills of poisonous
black gas. We could do nothing but wait during those long
weary hours.

I grew very weary of the curate's talking. After a time
I kept away from him, staying in a room by myself. But
he followed me there, so I went to another room at the
top of the house and locked myself in.

I kept thinking about my wife. I imagined her at
Leatherhead, frightened, in danger, believing me to be
dead. My cousin, I knew, was very brave, but he was not
the sort of man to realize the danger quickly. What was
needed now was not bravery, but thoughtful care. My only
hope was that the Martians were moving towards London
and away from them.

We were hopelessly surrounded by the black mist all
that Monday, and on the Tuesday morning. There had
been signs of people in the next house on Sunday night
— a face at the window and moving lights, and later the
banging of a door. But I do not know who these people
were, nor what happened to them. We saw nothing of
them the next day.

The black mist came nearer and nearer to us on Monday
morning, along the road outside the house in which we
were hiding. A Martian came across the fields about
midday. He had a machine which fired what looked like

super-heated steam. The steam hissed against the walls, smashed all the windows it touched, and burned the curate's hand as he ran out of the front room. It did, however, wash away all the black mist. At last we crept across the room and looked out again. Outside it looked as if a black snowstorm had passed over us. Looking towards the river, we were amazed to see a peculiar redness mixing with the black of the burned fields.

For a time we stayed where we were and then I decided that, as the black mist had gone, we could escape from this place. But the curate did not want to move.

'We are safe here,' he repeated, 'safe here.'

I decided to leave him — oh, if only I had! I looked for food and drink. I had already found oil and some pieces of clean cloth for my burns, and I also took a hat and a shirt that I found in one of the bedrooms. When the curate realized that I was going without him, he suddenly made up his mind to come too. And as all was quiet during the afternoon, we started out at about five o'clock, along the black road towards Sunbury.

Beyond Sunbury

In Sunbury there were many dead bodies — horses as well as people — broken carts and luggage, all covered thickly with black dust. We went on and reached Hampton Court in safety. After this we walked through Bushey Park. There were some horses there, feeding under the trees. Some men and women in the distance were the first living people we saw.

At Twickenham there was no sign of the damaging heat-ray, or the deadly black mist. There were more people here, but none had any news. Most of them were moving away, but there must have been some still left in their houses, too frightened to even run away.

We crossed Richmond Bridge at about half-past eight. We hurried across the bridge, of course, but I noticed

floating down the river a number of red shapes, some
many feet across. I did not know what these were and,
as there was no time to stop for a close look, I imagined
them to be more horrible than they really were. Here
again, on the Surrey side of the Thames, was black dust
that had once been mist, and dead bodies — some lying
in a heap near the entrance to the railway station. We did
not see any Martians there.

At Barnes we saw a group of three people in the
distance. They were running down a side street towards
the river, but there was no one else. Up the hill, Richmond
town was burning, but outside the town there was no sign
of the black mist.

A Martian captures some people

Then suddenly, as we approached Kew, a number of
people came running towards us, and the upper part of
a Martian fighting-machine came in sight over the tops of
the houses, less than a hundred yards away. We stood
still, shocked by the danger we were in. If the Martian
had looked down, he would have seen us, and we would
have been killed instantly. We were so frightened that we
dared not go on, but turned aside and hid in a shed in a
garden. There the curate sat, crying silently, and refusing
to move again.

But I was determined to reach Leatherhead and, as it
began to get dark, I went out again. I walked through
some bushes, and along a path beside a big house, and
came out on the road towards Kew. I left the curate in
the shed, but he came hurrying after me.

Setting out at that time was the most foolish thing I ever
did. For it was clear that the Martians were still around
us. The curate had only just caught up with me when we
saw either the fighting-machine we had seen before, or
another, far away across the fields. Four or five people
were hurrying along in front of it. In a moment we could

see that it was chasing them. In three steps it was among them, and they ran from its feet in all directions. The Martian did not use the heat-ray to destroy them, but picked them up one by one. It threw them into the great metal basket which hung on its back.

We stood for a moment, terror-struck, then turned and ran through a gate behind us into a walled garden, fell into a ditch, and lay there, scarcely daring to whisper to one another until the stars were out.

I suppose it was nearly eleven o'clock at night before we gathered courage to start again. This time we kept away from the road, and crept along the hedges and through gardens, watching for the Martians, who seemed to be all around us. In one place we found a burned and black area, now cooling, and a number of scattered dead bodies of men and horses. They were lying by a line of four smashed guns.

Sheen, it seemed, had escaped the destruction, but the place was silent and empty. Here my companion suddenly complained of feeling faint, and we decided to rest in one of the houses.

Food and shelter

In the first house we entered, after a little difficulty with the window, I found nothing to eat but a piece of bad cheese. There was, however, water to drink, and I took an axe which promised to be useful for breaking in to the next house we wanted to enter.

We crossed the
fields to a place
where the road turns
towards Mortlake. Here
there was a white house inside a
walled garden, and in the kitchen of this house we found
a store of food — two loaves of bread, an uncooked piece
of meat, and some ham. There were also some bottles of
beer, standing under a shelf, and two bags of beans and
some green vegetables. Next to the kitchen was a store-
room where there was firewood, and a cupboard in which
we found nearly a dozen bottles of red wine, tinned soups
and fish, and two tins of biscuits. I remember these details
very clearly because, as it happened, it was all we had to
live on for the next fortnight.

We sat in the adjacent kitchen in the dark — for we
dared not strike a light — and ate bread and ham, and
drank beer out of the same bottle. The curate, who was
still afraid and restless, now wanted to go on. I told him
to keep up his strength by eating. Then the thing which
was to keep us prisoners happened.

'It can't be midnight yet,' I said, and then at exactly that
moment there came a blinding green light. Everything in
the kitchen could be seen for a second, and then it all
disappeared again. And there followed such an explosion
as I have never heard before or since. Close after this came
a noise behind me, a crash of glass and falling bricks all
around us, and bits of the ceiling came down on us,

smashing into pieces on our heads. I was knocked across the floor where I hit my head against the handle of the oven door and became unconscious. I remained this way for a long time, the curate told me. When I recovered we were in darkness again, and the curate was wiping my face with water. 5

The fifth cylinder

For some time I could not remember what had happened. Then things came to me slowly, and I felt the lump on my head. 10

'Are you better?' asked the curate, in a whisper.

At last I answered him. I sat up.

'Don't move,' he said. 'The floor is covered with broken dishes. You can't possibly move without making a noise and I think they are outside.' 15

We both sat silent, so that we could scarcely hear one another breathing. Everything seemed deadly still though once something near us, some broken bricks or other building material, slid with a crash to the ground. Outside and very near was the rattle of metal. 20

'There!' said the curate, when presently it happened again.

'Yes,' I said. 'But what is it?'

'A Martian!' said the curate. I listened once more.

'It was not like the heat-ray,' I said. For a time I thought 25 that perhaps one of the great fighting-machines had stumbled against the house, as I had seen one stumble against the tower of Shepperton church.

For three or four hours, until the dawn came, we scarcely moved. And then the light came in, not through 30 the window, which remained black, but through a triangular hole between a piece of wood and a heap of broken bricks in the wall separating the kitchen from the house. We could now see the kitchen clearly for the first time. 35

The window had been burst in by a lot of garden soil, which was all over the floor. Outside, the soil was heaped up high against the house so no light could come in from that side at all. Sticking out of the soil, near the top of the window, we could see a broken water pipe. The floor was covered with smashed dishes. Daylight was shining in the hole in the wall, and through it we could see that the whole house was badly damaged. It seemed about to fall down.

As the dawn grew brighter, we saw, through the gap in the wall, a Martian standing outside. It was standing over a still-glowing cylinder. At this sight, we crawled as carefully as possible out of the dim kitchen and into the darkness of the store-room.

Suddenly I realized what had happened.

'The fifth cylinder,' I whispered, 'the fifth shot from Mars, has struck this house and buried us under the ruins!'

For a while we lay quite still in the store-room. I hardly dared to breathe, and sat with my eyes fixed on the faint light of the kitchen door. I could just see the curate's face, a dim shape, and his collar and shirt sleeves. A hammering noise began outside, and then, after a period of quiet, a hissing sound, like the hissing of an engine. These noises continued, and seemed to increase in number as the time went by. Presently a regular, much heavier noise began and continued. The floor seemed to be moving beneath our feet. For many hours we must have sat there, silent and trembling, until we fell asleep.

At last I woke up, very hungry. I think we must have slept for most of a day. I was so hungry that I told my companion I was going to get some food. He did not answer me, so I crept to the kitchen. But, as soon as I started eating, the faint noise I made reached him, and I heard him crawling after me.

INSIDE THE MARTIAN PIT

The view from the ruined house

After eating we crept back to the store-room and there I
must have slept again for, when I sat up and looked
around, I was alone. The heavy beating noise continued
steadily. I whispered for the curate several times, and at   5
last felt my way to the door of the kitchen. It was still
daylight, and I saw him across the room, lying by the
triangular hole that looked out upon the Martians. His
shoulders were raised, so that his head was hidden from
me.   10

I could hear a number of noises, almost like those of
a factory, and the place rocked with the beating noise.
Through the hole in the wall I could see the top of a tree,
and the warm blue of the evening sky. For a minute or
so I remained watching the curate, and then I advanced,   15
bending and stepping with extreme care amongst the
broken dishes that covered the floor.

I touched the curate's leg, and he jumped so violently
that some of the broken wall went sliding down outside
and fell with a loud noise. I held his arm, afraid that   20
he might cry out, and for a long time we sat without
moving. The falling wall had made the hole wider, and
by raising myself carefully, I was able to see out of
this gap into what had been a quiet road the night
before. Now, only a few hours later, it had completely   25
changed.

The fifth cylinder must have fallen right into the
middle of the first house we had visited. The building
had disappeared, completely smashed by the blow.

The cylinder lay deep in a hole, already much larger than the pit I had looked into at Woking. The earth all round it had splashed out when the cylinder landed — splashed is the only word I can use to describe it — and lay in heaped piles that hid dozens of houses near by. Our house had collapsed backwards; the front part, even on the ground floor, had been destroyed completely. Somehow, the kitchen and store-room had escaped, and stood buried now under soil and ruins, surrounded by tons of earth, except on the side where the cylinder was. On that side we were hanging on the very edge of the great circular pit the Martians were busy making. The heavy beating noise was evidently coming from machines quite close by, and sometimes a cloud of bright green smoke came up in front of us.

The cylinder in the centre of the pit had already opened and on the far edge of the pit stood one of the fighting-machines, empty, stiff and tall against the evening sky. But at first I scarcely noticed the pit or the cylinder. My attention was fixed on an extraordinary glittering machine I saw, busy working, and also on the strange creatures that were crawling slowly and painfully across a heap of earth near it.

I could not take my eyes off this new machine. It looked like a sort of metal crab with five jointed legs, and a lot of levers, bars, and tentacles all around its body. These metal arms could reach out and hold on to things. Most of the arms were pulled in at that moment, but with three long tentacles it was taking rods, metal plates and bars out of the cylinder, and placing them on the ground behind it.

It moved so quickly and perfectly that at first I did not think of it as a machine, in spite of its shiny surface. The fighting-machines were cleverly made, but nothing to compare with this. People who have never seen these machines, except in drawings, cannot realize how very alive they seemed.

The true Martians

At first, as I say, I did not think of this handling-machine
as a machine at all, but as a crab-like creature with a
glittering skin. The controlling Martian, whose tentacles
made it move, seemed to me to be the crab's brain. But   5
then I saw the Martian's damp, grey-brown skin and
noticed more of the creatures behind it, and I realized that
the glittering crab was not alive. It was a Martian machine.

I had already seen the Martians for a short time when
they came out of the first cylinder on Horsell Common.   10
Now that I was so close to their pit, but hidden from
them, I could have a really good look at them. They were
the most unearthly creatures it is possible to imagine.
They were huge round bodies or, rather, heads, about
four feet across. Each body had, in front of it, a face. This   15
face had no nose — the Martians did not seem to have
a sense of smell — but it had a pair of very large eyes,

and just beneath this a kind of fleshy beak. In the back of the head, or body, was the single ear. In a group round the mouth were sixteen whip-like tentacles, arranged in two bunches of eight each. These bunches have now been named the hands. As I saw the Martians properly for the first time, they were trying to lift themselves up on these hands but, of course, with the increased weight of earthly conditions, this was impossible. There is a possibility that, on Mars, they may have walked on these hands with no trouble at all.

It has since been discovered that inside, the larger part of the Martians was brain. Besides this there were lungs, for breathing, and a heart, and that was all. The Martians were heads, merely heads. They did not eat, so had no stomach. Instead, they took the fresh living blood of other creatures directly into their own blood. Later I saw this being done, as I shall describe. For now I shall just say that blood obtained from a still-living animal, in most cases from a human being, was run directly by means of a thin tube into the Martians' veins.

While I am describing the Martians, I will add more details which, although they were not all evident to us at that time, will help the reader to form a clearer picture of these dreadful creatures.

The Martians never went to sleep. They never got tired, and in twenty-four hours they would do twenty-four hours' work, just as the ants do on our Earth.

I think it is possible that many thousands of years ago the Martians may have been people not unlike ourselves. But they have developed the brain and hands, and the body has disappeared.

Their systems were different from ours in a simple but very important way. Dangerous bacteria, which cause so much disease and pain on earth, have either never appeared on Mars, or the Martians destroyed them all long ago. These Martians have never known dreadful diseases like we have.

Also, while speaking of the differences between life on Mars and life on Earth, I will mention here the Red Weed.

It seems that the vegetable kingdom on Mars, instead of having green for its main colour, has red. Anyway, the Martians brought seeds with them, which grew into red plants. Only one, known as the Red Weed, managed to grow for any length of time. It grew very quickly and strongly. It spread up the sides of the pit by the third or fourth day of our being kept prisoners there. Its thick branches formed a red border round the edges of our triangular window. And afterwards I found it had spread throughout the country, and especially wherever there was a stream of water.

While I was still watching their movements, and noticing every strange detail of their form, the curate reminded me that he was still there by pulling at my arm. He wanted to look out and, as there was only room for one of us at a time to watch, I gave up my place to him.

When I looked out again, the busy handling-machine had already joined together several pieces of the metal it had taken from the cylinder into a shape very like its own. And down on the left a busy little digging-machine had come into view, pouring out clouds of green smoke and working its way round the pit, digging and making banks of earth very carefully. This was what had caused the regular beating sound. It made little whistling noises as it worked. So far as I could see, it had no controlling Martian at all.

Human voices

The arrival of a second fighting-machine sent us quickly back into the store-room for we feared that, from its great height, the Martian might see us behind our wall. Even though it was very dangerous, we both kept creeping out from time to time to look through the gap. We could not stop ourselves wanting to find out what was happening

outside. And I remember how we struggled with each other, each wanting to be the first to look out. We would race across the kitchen, eager, and yet afraid of making a noise, and strike each other, and push and kick, all within
5   a few inches of being seen. And while we fought in whispers, and hurriedly ate and drank, outside in the hot sun of that terrible June, the Martians were busy in their pit.

Three more fighting-machines had arrived and brought
10   with them some new machines. The difference between the quick and clever movements of these machines and the clumsiness of their masters was great, and I had to keep telling myself that it was the masters that were the living things.

15   The curate was watching through the hole when the first people were brought to the pit. I was sitting below, listening hard. He made a sudden movement backwards and came sliding down the rubbish. He sat beside me in the darkness, quite unable to speak, waving his hands
20   and, for a moment, I shared his terror. He waved towards the hole in the wall and, after a little while, my curiosity gave me courage. I got up, stepped across him, and climbed up to it. At first I could not see the reason for his terror. It was nearly dark and the stars were little and faint,
25   but the pit was lit by a greenish fire. The true Martians were nowhere to be seen and a fighting-machine, with its legs pulled in and shortened, stood across the corner of the pit. And then, through the noise of the machinery, came the sound of human voices.

30   ## The Martian feeds

I sat watching this fighting-machine closely, and I could see now, for the first time, that the hood did contain a Martian. As the green flames lifted I could see the oily gleam of his skin and the brightness of his eyes. And
35   suddenly I heard a scream, and saw a long tentacle

reaching over the machine to the basket that hung from its back. Then something — something struggling violently — was lifted up against the sky and, as this black object came down again, I saw by the green brightness that it was a man. For an instant I saw him clearly. He was rather 5 fat, middle-aged and well dressed. I could see his staring eyes and gleams of light shining on his watch-chain. He disappeared behind a heap of earth, and for a moment there was silence. Then a terrible screaming began, which went on for many long, terrifying minutes. And from the 10 Martian came a cheerful hooting sound.

I slid down the rubbish, struggled to my feet, put my hands over my ears and ran into the store-room. The curate, who had been sitting silently with his arms over his head, looked up as I passed, cried to me not to leave 15 him alone, and came running after me.

That night I tried without success to think of a plan of escape. The curate was no longer able to discuss things sensibly. He behaved at times like an animal. I was desperate to get away. I thought our best chance was the 20 possibility that the Martians would leave this pit at some time, and that they might not consider it necessary to leave someone behind to guard it. I thought very carefully about the possibility of our digging a way out in a direction away from the pit. But the chances of our 25 coming up within sight of a fighting-machine seemed too enormous. Also, the curate certainly would not have helped me to dig.

On the third day, if I remember correctly, I saw another person killed — a young man this time. It was the only 30 occasion on which I actually saw the Martians feed. After that, I avoided the hole in the wall for nearly a day. I went into the store-room and spent some hours digging with my axe as silently as possible. However, when I had made a hole about two feet deep, the loose earth collapsed 35 noisily, and I did not dare continue. I was disappointed, and lay down on the store-room floor for a long time.

After that I gave up altogether the idea of escaping by digging a tunnel.

At first I thought it would be impossible for us to escape from the Martians through the help of other human beings. But on the fourth or fifth night I heard a sound like heavy guns.

It was very late at night, and the moon was shining brightly. The Martians had taken away the digging-machine and, except for a fighting-machine that stood on the far side of the pit, and a handling-machine that was busy somewhere out of my sight, there was nothing else there at all.

I heard a dog howling, and the noise was so familiar that it made me listen. Then I heard quite clearly a noise exactly like the sound of great guns. Six clear shots I counted and, after a long silence, six more. And that was all.

THE NOISES STOP

The curate must speak

It was on the sixth day of our imprisonment that I looked through the hole for the last time. Presently I found myself alone. The curate was no longer sitting close to me, trying to take my place at the gap, but had gone back into the store-room. I had a sudden thought, and went back quickly and quietly to find him. In the darkness I heard the curate drinking. I put out my hand in the darkness, and my fingers touched a wine bottle.

For a few minutes there was a struggle. The bottle struck the floor and broke. I stopped fighting and got up. We stood breathing hard, threatening one another. In the end I placed myself between him and the food, and told him that he must not steal it. There was not a lot left and we must be careful with it, or we should very soon be starving. I divided the food in the kitchen into daily amounts, and would not let him have any more that day. There was just enough to last for ten more days.

In the afternoon he tried to steal some food. I had been half asleep but, in an instant, I was awake. All day and all night we sat face to face. I was weary but determined, and he was weeping and complaining of his hunger.

For two days we struggled with each other. There were times when I beat and kicked him madly, times when I argued with him, trying to make him be sensible. He would not give up his attacks on the food, and he never stopped talking to himself. Slowly I began to realize that my only companion in this terrible adventure was completely mad.

On the eighth day he began to talk loudly instead of in a whisper, and nothing I could do would make him keep quiet.

Then he suddenly remembered the food I was keeping from him, and he asked for it, praying, weeping and at last threatening. He began to raise his voice. I asked him not to. He threatened that if I did not give him food he would shout and let the Martians know where we were. For a time that frightened me, but if I had given in to him there would not have been enough food to last. So I refused him, although I was afraid he might do as he had promised. But that day, anyway, he did not. He talked with his voice rising slowly, through most of the eighth and ninth days. Then he slept for a time and when he woke up, he began again so loudly that I had to make him stop.

'Be silent!' I said angrily.

He rose to his knees, for he had been sitting on the floor.

'I have been silent too long,' he said, so loudly that he must have been heard in the pit, 'and now I must speak. I must speak!'

'Shut up!' I said, rising to my feet, and in terror in case the Martians should hear us. 'Keep your voice down!' I hissed in an angry whisper.

'No!' shouted the curate at the top of his voice, standing with his arms stretched out. 'I must speak!'

In three steps he was at the door into the kitchen.

'I must speak. I must go. I have been silent for too long.'

I put out my hand and felt the meat-axe hanging on the wall. In a flash I was after him. I was mad with fear. Before he was halfway across the kitchen I had caught up with him. I turned the blade of the axe back and struck him with the other end. He fell forward and lay stretched on the ground. I tripped over him, and stood breathing hard. He lay still.

We are discovered!

Suddenly I heard a noise from outside, and the crash of a wall coming down. The triangular hole in the kitchen wall went black. I looked up and saw the lower part of a handling-machine coming slowly across the gap. One of its metal arms curled among the rubbish; another arm appeared, feeling its way over the fallen bricks. I stood in terror, staring. Then I saw, through a sort of glass plate near the edge of the body, the face and large dark eyes of a Martian. Then a long metal snake-like tentacle came feeling slowly through the hole.

I turned, tripped over the curate again, and stopped by the store-room door. The tentacle was now two yards or more into the kitchen, and twisting this way and that with sudden movements. With a faint cry, I turned and ran across the store-room. I trembled violently; I could scarcely stand up. I opened the door of the coal cellar, and stood there in the darkness, staring at the faintly lit doorway into the kitchen, and listening. Had the Martian seen me? What was it doing now?

Something was moving about in the kitchen, very quietly. Every now and then it tapped against the wall, or started its movements with a faint ringing sound, like a bunch of keys on a chain. Then I heard something heavy — I knew too well what — being slowly pulled across the floor of the kitchen towards the opening. I crept to the door and looked into the kitchen. In the triangle of sunlight I saw the Martian in its handling-machine, examining the curate's head. I thought at once that it would know somebody else was there because of the mark of the blow I had given him.

I crept back to the coal cellar and shut the door. In the darkness I began trying to cover myself up as much as I could among the firewood and coal, and as silently as possible. Every now and then I stopped to hear if the Martian had pulled its tentacle back through the opening.

Then the faint ringing began again. I imagined it slowly feeling its way over the kitchen. Presently I heard it nearer — in the store-room. I thought that it might not be long enough to reach me. I prayed all the time. It passed, scraping faintly across the coal cellar door. Then I heard it trying to lift up the latch. It had found the door! The Martian understood doors and latches!

It played with the latch for a minute, perhaps, and then the door opened.

In the darkness I could just see the thing waving towards me and touching and examining the walls, coals, firewood, and ceiling. It was like a large blind black snake swaying its head to and fro.

Once, it touched the heel of my boot. I was on the point of screaming; I bit my hand. For a time it was silent. I thought it had gone. But presently, with a loud noise, it picked up something — I thought it had me! Then it seemed to go out of the cellar again. For a minute I was not sure. It seemed to have taken a lump of coal to examine.

I moved my position slightly, for I was most uncomfortable, and listened. I whispered prayers for my safety.

Then I heard the slow, steady sound creeping towards me again. Slowly, slowly it drew nearer, scratching against walls and tapping the floor.

While I was still wondering if I was about to die, it knocked against the cellar door and closed it. I heard it go into the kitchen. The biscuit tins rattled, a bottle smashed, and then there was a heavy bang. Then silence.

Had it gone?

At last I decided that it had.

It did not come into the store-room again; but I lay all the tenth day, in the darkness, buried among the coal and firewood, not daring even to crawl out for a drink. It was the eleventh day before I came out from my hiding-place.

The stillness

The first thing I did was to search the store-room for food. But it was empty; every bit of food had gone. The Martian must have taken it all the day before. At that discovery I lost hope for the first time. I had no food and nothing to drink on the eleventh day.

At first my mouth and throat were dry, and I felt my strength leaving me. I sat in the darkness of the store-room, feeling very sorry for myself. All I could think about was food. I thought I had become deaf, for I had been used to hearing the noise of movements from the pit, and this had stopped absolutely. I did not feel strong enough to crawl noiselessly to the gap in the wall, or I would have gone there.

On the twelfth day my throat was so painful that I used the water-pump which stood by the sink. I managed to get a cup or two of blackened rain-water. I felt much better after this, especially as no inquiring tentacle came to find out what had caused the noise of my pumping. During these days I thought a lot about the curate, and the way in which he had died.

On the thirteenth day I drank some more water, slept a little, and thought of eating and plans of escape. When I slept I had the most horrible dreams, of the death of the curate, or of wonderful dinners. But, sleeping or awake, I felt a pain that urged me to drink again and again. The light that came into the store-room was no longer grey but red. To my wild imagination it seemed the colour of blood.

On the fourteenth day I went into the kitchen, and I was surprised to find that the red weed had grown right across the hole in the wall, making everything look red.

It was early on the fifteenth day that I heard a curious noise from the kitchen and, listening, recognized it as the scratching of a dog. I went into the kitchen and saw a dog's nose through a break among the red weed. This greatly surprised me. At the scent of me he barked.

I thought that if I could persuade him to come into the place quietly I should be able, perhaps, to kill him and eat him. Anyhow, it would be a good idea to kill him in case he attracted the attention of the Martians.

I crept forward, saying, 'Good dog!' very softly; but he suddenly pulled back his head and disappeared.

I listened — I was not deaf — but certainly the pit was quiet. For a long while I lay close to the hole in the wall, but did not dare to move aside the red plants that covered it. Once or twice I heard a faint noise like the feet of the dog going backwards and forwards on the sand far below me, and there was also the sound of birds, but that was all. At last, encouraged by the silence, I looked out.

The empty pit

Except in the corner, where some large black birds were fighting noisily over the bones of the dead people on which the Martians had fed, there was not a living thing in the pit.

I stared about me, scarcely believing my eyes. All the machinery had gone. There was a heap of greyish-blue powder in one corner, and in another, a few metal bars, the birds and the bones of the dead, but nothing else at all. The place was merely an empty circular pit in the sand.   5

Slowly I crawled out through the red weed, and stood up on the heap of rubbish. I could see in all directions, except behind me. There were no Martians to be seen. The pit was directly beneath my feet, but a little way along, the rubbish made a slope to the top of the ruins.   10 My chance of escape had come. I began to tremble.

I hesitated for a time, and then, with my heart beating loudly, I climbed up to the top of the heap in which I had been buried for so long. I looked about again. Behind me, too, there was still no sign of the Martians.   15

When I had last seen this part of Sheen in the daylight, it had been a long street of comfortable white and red houses, with trees here and there. Now I stood on a heap of smashed bricks, clay and gravel. Over all this rubbish spread hundreds of red plants, knee high. The trees near   20 me were dead and brown, but had red creepers climbing along their branches.

The neighbouring houses had all been wrecked, but none had been burned. The windows were smashed, the doors broken and the roofs damaged. The red weed grew   25 in their rooms. Below me was the great pit, with the large birds struggling over its rubbish. A number of smaller birds hopped about among the ruins. Far away I saw a starved cat, but there were no signs of living people anywhere.

I had been in the dark for so long that the daylight   30 seemed almost blindingly bright, and the sky was a glowing blue. A gentle wind kept the red weed, that covered every bit of empty ground, gently swaying. And oh, how sweet the fresh air was!

12

THE CRYING MARTIAN

The work of fifteen days

For some time I stood on the top of the heap of earth, not thinking of my safety. Inside that horrible prison, from which I had just escaped, I had thought only about myself. I had not realized what had been happening to the world. I had not imagined how different everywhere would be. I had expected to see Sheen in ruins, but not like this. It was like looking at another planet, not like our own familiar world at all.

In the direction away from the pit, I saw, on the far side of a red-covered wall, a patch of garden which was still clear. This gave me an idea. I walked through the red weed. Sometimes it came up to my knees, and at other times it was up to my neck. It gave me a comfortable feeling of being hidden. When I reached the garden wall I found it was six feet high. I tried to climb over it, but I was too weak to lift my feet to the top. So I walked along beside it, and came to a corner where I found a rock. I stood on it, climbed over the wall, and so got into the garden. Growing here I found some young onions and a quantity of carrots, and I took them all to eat. I climbed over a low wall and went on my way towards Kew. I walked through an avenue of red trees, and it was like walking through an avenue of drops of blood.

I now had two main ideas, to get more food, and to move, as soon and as far as my strength allowed, out of this awful, unearthly region around the pit.

A little way on, in a grassy place, I found some bushes with fruit growing on them, which I also ate. Then I saw a brown sheet of water where fields used to be. At first

I was surprised at this flood in a hot, dry summer, but afterwards I discovered that it was caused by the fast-growing red weed. As soon as this extraordinary plant met water, it at once became enormous. Its seeds poured down into the water of the rivers Wey and Thames, and its fast-growing, thick stems soon choked both rivers, making the water flow all over the banks into the fields.

At Putney, as I saw later, the bridge was almost lost underneath this weed, and at Richmond, too, the Thames water poured in a broad and shallow stream across the fields of Hampton and Twickenham. As the waters spread, the weed followed them, until the ruined houses of the Thames Valley were for a time lost in this great lake of red plants.

In the end, the red weed died almost as quickly as it spread. A disease, caused, it is believed, by the action of certain bacteria, destroyed it. All earthly plants can resist diseases of this kind — they never give in without a severe struggle; but the red weed rotted like a thing already dead. The stems became white, and then dry. They broke off at the slightest touch, and the waters which had encouraged their growth carried the last bits of them out to sea.

Of course, as soon as I came to this water, I wanted to drink. I drank quite a lot, and even tried to eat some of the red weed, but it had a nasty taste. I walked through the water towards Mortlake. Here and there a ruined house, or a fence, or a street-lamp, pointed out the road to me. And so presently I got out of this flood and made my way up a hill, and came out on Putney Common.

Putney Common

Here the scenery changed again. It was no longer strange and unknown, but wrecked and familiar. Some patches of ground looked as though they had suffered from a severe

storm, and then I would find a group of houses quite
undamaged, with their curtains drawn and doors closed,
as if they had been left for the day by their owners. The
red weed did not grow so thickly here, and the tall trees
along the road were free from red creepers. I hunted for
food among the trees, finding nothing, and I also went
into two or three silent houses, but people had been there
before me, and everything had gone. I stopped for the
rest of that day hidden in some bushes. I was too tired to
go on.

All this time I saw no human beings, and no signs of
the Martians. I met some hungry-looking dogs, but they
hurried away as soon as they saw me going towards them.
I found two human skeletons, their bones dry and white
and without a scrap of flesh or skin upon them. Later, in
a wood, I found some bones of cats and rabbits. I was so
hungry that I sucked several of these, but there was
nothing to be got from them.

After sunset, I struggled along the road towards Putney,
where I think the heat-ray must have been used for some
reason. And in one garden I found some potatoes. From
this garden I could look down to Putney and the river.
Everywhere there were black trees, black ruins and, down
the hill, the flooded river, which was red with the Martians'
weed. And over everything, there was complete silence.
It filled me with terror to think how quickly that change
had come.

For a time I believed that mankind had been swept out
of existence here, and that I must be the last man still
alive. At the top of Putney Hill I found more human bones,
and became more and more certain that, except for a few
lucky ones like myself who had somehow managed to
escape, the Martians had already killed everyone in
this part of the world. They had gone on, I thought, to
find their food somewhere else. Perhaps even now they
were destroying Berlin or Paris, or maybe they had gone
northward.

Dead London

I spent that night in the hotel that stands at the top of Putney Hill, sleeping comfortably in a bed for the first time since my journey to Leatherhead began. I searched for food, and at last found a piece of bread, already half-eaten 5 by rats, and two tins of pineapple. The place had been searched before, and any other food had been taken.

I did not dare to light a lamp, for I was afraid that I might attract the attention of the Martians. Before I went to bed I went from window to window, looking out for 10 some sign of these monsters. I slept very little because I kept thinking about the death of the curate, about where the Martians might be, and about what had happened to my wife.

The morning was bright and fine, and the eastern sky 15 glowed pink with little golden clouds. In the road that goes from the top of Putney Hill to Wimbledon were signs of the mad crowd that must have poured towards London on the Sunday night after the fighting started. There was a little two-wheeled cart painted with the name of Thomas 20 Lobb, New Malden, with a smashed wheel and an abandoned tin box. There was a hat that had been stamped into the mud, now dry and hard.

I had an idea of going to Leatherhead, though I knew that there was not much chance of finding my wife. 25 Certainly, unless they had all been killed very suddenly, my cousins and she would have moved from there. But perhaps if I went to Leatherhead someone might be able to tell me where they had gone.

I walked to the edge of the common. There was no red 30 weed to be seen, and still no sign of the Martians. I crossed the common and went down the hill to the bridge across the river. Here the red weed was growing, fast and strong. It nearly choked the road to the bridge, but it was already turning white in patches as the disease, which later 35 killed it, spread over its stems.

There was black dust along the road from the bridge, and it grew thicker in Fulham. The streets were horribly quiet. I got some food — though it was not very good — in a baker's shop there. As I journeyed on towards Walham Green the streets became clear of powder, and I passed a row of houses on fire. The noise of the burning was an absolute relief. Going on towards Brompton, the streets were quiet again.

Once again, in Brompton, I saw the black powder in the streets, and there were dead bodies, too. I saw about a dozen. They had been dead many days, and I hurried quickly past them. The black powder covered them, and one or two had been disturbed by dogs.

Where there was no black powder, it was curiously like a Sunday, with the closed shops, the houses locked up and the curtains drawn, the emptiness and the stillness. In some places the shops had been broken into, but rarely those which did not sell food. A jeweller's window had been broken open in one place, but the thief must have been disturbed, for a number of gold chains and a watch were scattered on the pavement. I did not touch them.

Unearthly howling

It was near South Kensington that I first heard the howling. It was not the same as before, just two notes, crying continually, 'Ulla, ulla, ulla, ulla.' When I passed streets

that ran to the north, it grew louder, and then the houses
and buildings seemed to cut it off again. It was loudest
down Exhibition Road. I stopped, staring towards
Kensington Gardens, wondering at this strange noise.

'Ulla, ulla, ulla, ulla,' cried that unearthly note. I turned
towards the iron gates of Hyde Park. I thought I might go
into the church there, and climb to the top to see out over
the park, but then I decided it was better to stay on the
ground where I could hide quickly if necessary. So I went
on up Exhibition Road. All the large houses there were
empty and still, and the sound of my footsteps echoed
from walls on either side of the road. I crossed the bridge
over the Serpentine. The voice grew stronger and stronger,
though I could see nothing above the house-tops on the
north side of the park.

'Ulla, ulla, ulla, ulla,' cried the voice, coming, it seemed
to me, from the district around Regent's Park.

It was already past noon. Why, I asked myself, was I
wandering alone in this city of the dead?

I came to Oxford Street by Marble Arch, and here again
I saw black powder and several bodies. There was also
an evil smell which came from the cellars of some of the
houses. I grew very thirsty after the heat of my long walk.
With great trouble I managed to break into a hotel and
get food and drink. I was weary after eating, and went
into one of the rooms to sleep.

When I woke up I heard that sad howling once more,
'Ulla, ulla, ulla, ulla.' It was now getting dark and, after I
had discovered some biscuits and cheese, I wandered on
through the houses to Baker Street, and came at last to
Regent's Park. I saw, far away over the trees, the hood of
the Martian giant from which this sad howling came. I
watched him for some time, but he did not move. He
seemed to be standing and crying, for no reason that I
could discover.

I tried to make a plan of action. That continuous
sound of 'Ulla, ulla, ulla, ulla,' confused my thinking.

Perhaps I was too tired to be very afraid. Certainly I was very curious to know the reason for this crying. I turned back, away from the park, and went along under the shelter of houses until I got a view of this Martian from the direction of St. John's Wood. Suddenly I heard barking and saw first a dog with a piece of rotting red meat in his mouth coming towards me, and then more starving dogs chasing him. As the barking died away down the road, the sound of 'Ulla, ulla, ulla, ulla,' began again.

I found a wrecked handling-machine halfway to St. John's Wood station, amongst the ruins of a house. At first I thought the house had fallen across the road. It was only as I climbed among the ruins that I saw, in surprise, this mechanical giant lying with its tentacles bent and smashed and twisted among the ruins it had made. It looked as if it had driven blindly straight into the house, and had been smashed as the house fell. It seemed to me then that this might have been caused by a handling-machine escaping from the control of its Martian. I could not climb down among the ruins to see the machine, and it was now too dark to see inside it.

Wondering still more at all I had seen, I went on towards Primrose Hill. Far away, through a gap in the trees, I saw a second Martian, as still as the first, standing silently in the park. A little way on from the smashed handling-machine I found the red weed again, and Regent's Canal was thick with it.

As I crossed the bridge, the howling began again. 'Ulla, ulla, ulla, ul …'. It stopped quite suddenly, as if it had been cut off.

THE TERROR IS OVER

Dead!

The houses about me stood faint, and tall, and dim; the trees towards the park were growing black. All about me the red weed climbed among the ruins. Night was coming on. While that voice had sounded, I had not felt so alone. But now I was very frightened. The road in front of me became black, and I saw a twisted shape lying on the pavement. I could not make myself go on. I turned down St John's Wood Road, and ran from this awful stillness towards Kilburn. I hid until long after midnight, in a hut in the Harrow Road. But before dawn my courage returned, and while the stars were still in the sky, I turned once more towards Regent's Park.

I lost my way among the streets, and presently saw, down a long avenue, in the half-light of the early morning, the curve of Primrose Hill. On the top of the hill was a third Martian, as still as the others I had seen, and just as silent.

A mad idea came into my head. I would die and end it all. And I would save myself even the trouble of killing myself. I marched towards this giant, and then, as I got nearer and the light increased, I saw that a crowd of large black birds was gathering round the hood. At that sight my heart leapt, and I began running along the road.

As the sun rose, I came out at the bottom of Primrose Hill. Looking up, I could see great heaps of earth at the top, making a sort of wall. This was the final and largest pit the Martians made. From behind these heaps a thin smoke rose up to the sky. A dog ran along the top of the hill and disappeared. The thought that had flashed into

my mind grew real, grew possible. I felt no fear, only a
wild trembling happiness, as I ran up the hill towards the
silent monster. I looked up at its hood. Something was
different. Something was wrong. Out of the front of the
5   hood hung long ragged greyish brown strips on which the
hungry birds were feeding.

In another moment I had climbed up to the top of the
heaps, and stood looking down into the pit. It was a huge
space, with enormous machines here and there inside it.
10   And scattered about it, some in their wrecked handling-
machines, some in other war-machines, and a dozen of
them laid in a row, were the Martians — dead! — killed
by the bacteria against which their systems were
unprepared; killed as the red weed was being killed;
15   killed, after all mankind's efforts had failed, by some of
the smallest inhabitants of this earth.

There were nearly fifty altogether in the great pit they
had made. At that time, of course, I did not know why
they had died. I only knew that these things that had been
20   alive and so terrible to people were dead.

I stood staring into the pit. The huge machines, so great
and wonderful in their power, so unearthly in their shapes,
rose out of the shadows, dim and strange. A crowd of
dogs fought over the bodies that lay in the bottom of the
25   pit, far below me. Across on the other side of the pit, huge
and strange, lay a great flying-machine. They must have
been building this when decay and death stopped them.
At the sound of the birds overhead I looked up at the
huge fighting-machine that would fight no more.

30   I turned and looked down the slope of the hill. I could
see the two other war-machines standing where their
Martians had died. They glittered now, harmless tripod
towers of shining metal, in the brightness of the rising sun.

All about the pit, and saved from complete destruction,
35   stretched the great City of London. The terror was over.
Even that day the healing would begin. The survivors
scattered over the country — without law, without leaders,

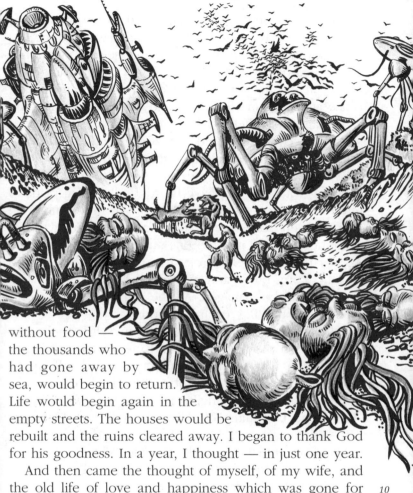

without food —
the thousands who
had gone away by
sea, would begin to return.
Life would begin again in the
empty streets. The houses would be
rebuilt and the ruins cleared away. I began to thank God
for his goodness. In a year, I thought — in just one year.

And then came the thought of myself, of my wife, and
the old life of love and happiness which was gone for   10
ever.

Good news

Now comes the strangest thing in my story. And yet,
perhaps, it is not altogether strange. I remember, clearly,
all that I did that day until the time I stood crying and   15
praising God upon the top of Primrose Hill. And then I
forget.

I know nothing of what happened to me in the next three days. I have found out since that I was not the first to discover the death of the Martians. Several others like myself had discovered them the night before, while I was hiding in the hut, one man had gone to the main post office at St. Martin's-le-Grand, and had managed to send a message from there to Paris. Quickly, the joyful news spread all over the world. They knew of it in Dublin, Edinburgh, Manchester, Birmingham, at the time when I stood on the edge of the pit. Already people were shouting with joy, so I have heard, and making plans to return to London. Church bells began to ring again. Men and women rode on bicycles down country lanes, shouting the good news to one another. And as for food! Across the Channel, across the Irish Sea, across the Atlantic, corn, bread and meat were being sent to us as fast as could be managed. All the shipping in the world seemed to be going towards London.

I didn't know any of this. I found myself in the house of kindly people who had found me on the third day. I had been wandering about, crying and talking to myself, in the streets of St. John's Wood. They have told me since that I was singing a stupid song, something about 'The Last Man Left Alive, Hurrah! The Last Man Left Alive.'

I was sick, and they were kind to me. When I was better again, they told me what had happened in Leatherhead. Two days after I had been trapped in the wrecked house at Sheen, Leatherhead had been destroyed, with everybody in it, by a Martian. I stayed with these kind people for four days after my recovery. All that time I felt that I wanted to look once more at the place where I had been so happy with my wife. They tried to persuade me not to go. But at last I could resist it no longer and, promising faithfully to return to see them, I went out again into the streets that had recently been so dark and strange and empty.

Already they were busy with returning people. In some places there were even shops open. I remember how bright the day seemed as I went back to the little house at Maybury Hill. So many people were out everywhere that it seemed unbelievable that any great number of the population had been killed.

The journey home

I saw very little of the damage that the Martians had done until I came to Waterloo Bridge. Here the red weed climbed all over the sides. At Waterloo station I found out about the free trains that were taking people back to their homes. Many had already gone and there were few people on the train I went on. I did not want to talk, so I found a part of the train where nobody else was sitting. I sat looking out at the destruction as we passed by.

All the way the countryside looked strange; black grass and trees were everywhere, and every little stream was blocked with the red weed. Beyond Wimbledon were the heaps of earth around the sixth cylinder. A number of people were standing around it, and some soldiers were busy in the middle of the pit. Over it, the British flag waved cheerfully in the wind.

The railway line on the London side of Woking was still being repaired, so I got off the train at Byfleet. I walked down the road to Maybury, past the place where the soldier and I had talked to the officer and on past the spot where I had seen my first Martian in the thunderstorm. Here I turned aside to look at the side of the road, and found the broken cart and the white bones of the horse. For a time I stood looking.

Then I returned through the woods, neck-high with red weed here and there, and found that the owner of the Spotted Dog had already been buried. A man standing at an open cottage door greeted me by name as I passed.

I looked at my house with a quick flash of hope that faded immediately. The door had been forced open, it was unfastened, and was opening slowly as I approached.

5 The wind banged it shut again. At the open window from which the soldier and I had watched the dawn, the curtains of my study moved a little. No one had closed that window since. Everything was just as I had left it four weeks ago. I went into the hall, and the place felt empty.

10 The stair carpet was dirty where I had sat on it, wet with rain, on the night I returned from Leatherhead. Our muddy footsteps, I saw, still went up the stairs.

I went into the dining-room. There were the meat and the bread, both very decayed, just as we had left them.

15 My home was empty. I saw how stupid I had been to hope that anybody would be there.

And then a strange thing happened. 'It is no use,' said a voice. 'The house is empty. No one has been here for days. Do not stay here making yourself unhappy. No one

20 has escaped but you.'

I jumped. Had I spoken my thoughts aloud? I turned, and the garden door was open behind me. I went to it and stood looking out.

And there, amazed and afraid, just as I was amazed

25 and afraid, were my cousins and my wife — my wife, her face white and looking very fearful. She gave a faint cry.

'I came,' she said. 'I knew — knew —'

She put her hand to her throat — swayed. I stepped

30 towards her, and caught her in my arms.

Unanswered questions

Now that I am ending my story, I am sorry that I cannot help in the discussion of many questions which are still unanswered. My own special subject is the study of the

35 mind, and I know little of medicine, except what I have

read in a book or two. But it seems to me that Carver's suggestions as to the reason of the rapid death of the Martians is so probable that it must be the truth.

In all the bodies of the Martians that were examined after the war, no bacteria except those already known to be on Earth were found. So it seems that they must have died after being attacked by our earthly bacteria.

No one knows what the black mist was made from, and how the heat-ray worked is still a puzzle. The black powder was examined and results of tests showed that it contained something unknown, which acts at once, with deadly effect, on the blood.

None of the brown liquid that floated down the Thames after the destruction of Shepperton was examined at the time, and now there is none left.

I have already told you the results of the examination of the Martians. There was not much of them to examine after the dogs had found them, but one was discovered almost complete, and is now kept in the Natural History Museum, for all to see.

The most serious question of all is whether the Martians will attack us again. I do not think that nearly enough attention is being given to this problem.

We should be prepared. It should be possible to find the exact position of the gun on Mars which fired the cylinders at the Earth. We should keep a continual watch on that part of the planet, and be ready for the next attack. Then the cylinders might be destroyed before they are cool enough for the Martians to leave them. Or the Martians might be killed with guns as soon as the top opens. It seems to me that they have lost a great advantage in the failure of their first attack. Perhaps they realize this too.

We have learnt now that this planet of ours is no longer the safe place we had thought it to be. We can never know the unseen good or evil that may come to us suddenly out of space.

It may be that from across the miles of space the
Martians on Mars watched the failure of their first attempt
to take the Earth from us, and have learnt their lesson.
However, for many years to come, Mars will certainly be
watched very carefully. And every time we see a falling
star we shall begin to feel afraid.

I must confess that the danger of those terrible days has
left a sense of doubt and uncertainty in my mind. I sit in
my study, writing by the light of a lamp, and suddenly I
see again in my mind the valley below, covered with
flames, and I feel the house to be empty around me. I go
out into the Byfleet road, and vehicles pass me; a boy in
a cart; a car full of visitors; a workman on a bicycle;
children going to school; and suddenly they become dim
and unreal, and I hurry again with the soldier through the
hot, still silence. At night I dream about the black powder
lying on the streets, and the bodies covered by it. They
rise up towards me and I wake, cold and frightened, in
the darkness.

I go to London and see the busy crowds in Fleet Street
and the Strand, and I think to myself that they are but
ghosts of the past, going to and fro in the streets which I
have seen silent and empty. And it is strange, too, to stand
on Primrose Hill. I was there the day before writing this
last chapter. The houses for miles around have been
rebuilt, people walk among the flower-beds on the hill,
and stop to stare at the Martian fighting-machine that is
still standing there. And as I stood there, listening to the
sound of children playing, I remembered it as I saw it
before, bright and hard and silent, under the dawn of that
last great day.

Strangest of all is to hold my wife's hand again, and to
think that once I counted her, and she counted me, among
the dead.

QUESTIONS AND ACTIVITIES

CHAPTER 1

Choose the right words to say what this part of the chapter is about.

Ogilvy thought a (1) **meteorite/planet** had fallen on Horsell Common. When he saw it, he was (2) **surprised/frightened** by its (3) **size/colour**. It was thirty (4) **inches/yards** across. He also expected it to be (5) **square/round**. The uncovered part looked like a huge (6) **box/cylinder**. He heard a (7) **loud/slight** noise. The top was turning. Then he knew that the cylinder was (8) **hollow/solid**.

CHAPTER 2

Some of these descriptions of a Martian are true and some are false. What is wrong with the false ones?

1 He was greenish, and about the size of a large bear.
2 His skin gleamed like the thick, wet skin of a fish.
3 He had two huge, light-coloured, staring eyes.
4 His mouth was trembling and dripping wet.
5 The lower lip of the mouth was V-shaped.
6 There were grey, snake-like tentacles around the eyes.
7 There was no chin below the lower lip.
8 He moved about quickly and painfully.

CHAPTER 3

Put the letters of these words in the right order.

It was 8.30 in the evening. A (1) **drowc** was standing near the sand pits watching the (2) **gninsnip** mirror. They saw what happened to the (3) **unattopied**. The (4) **rat-haye** came towards the crowd. They heard a (5) **ginswilth** noise, and then the (6) **emba** swung over them. Burning (7) **selave** fell onto the road and the people's (8) **costhel** began to catch fire.

CHAPTER 4

These sentences describe the object that the narrator saw. Put the beginnings with the right endings.

1	It was a walking machine	(a)	in long, easy steps.
2	It was four or five times	(b)	of glittering metal.
3	It strode over the tallest trees	(c)	shot out from its joints.
4	There were long tentacles	(d)	higher than the houses.
5	The hood on top	(e)	sounding like 'Aloo, aloo'.
6	Behind the main body was	(f)	moved around like a head.
7	Clouds of green smoke	(g)	rattling about its body.
8	It made deafening noises	(h)	a huge basket of white metal.

CHAPTER 5

Put the place-names in the right gaps. Choose from: **Weybridge, Leatherhead, Newhaven, Esher.**

The narrator wanted to go to (1) _____. He planned to take his wife to (2) _____, and go out of the country. The narrator decided to go with the soldier as far as (3) _____. Then he planned to go the long way round, through (4) _____ to reach (5) _____.

CHAPTER 6

Put these sentences in the right order to say what happened in the story. The first one is done for you.

1 A Martian went near Shepperton and raised its heat ray.
2 The monster smashed into Shepperton church tower.
3 The hood was torn off in a dozen pieces.
4 Water, steam, mud and metal shot far up into the sky.
5 Six guns, hidden on the edge of the village, fired at it.
6 A violent explosion shook the air.
7 Then it fell with a loud crash into the river.
8 The hood turned, and the fourth shell burst in its face.
9 The first three shells exploded near it.

CHAPTER 7

The (b) sentences in these paragraphs are in the wrong place. Where should they go?

1 (a) The Martians had black tubes which they fired, like guns. (b) <u>It looked like a small, dark, round hill.</u> (c) There was no explosion when the things they fired hit the ground.

2 (a) The narrator saw something towards Sudbury. (b) <u>The Martians fired their black tubes again.</u> (c) It grew lower and broader as he watched.

3 (a) Everything suddenly became still. (b) <u>The drums let out a cloud of gas that sank and spread out.</u> (c) This time, the army did not fire back at them.

4 (a) The Martians fired drums that smashed when they hit the ground. (b) <u>There was a bang, but no flash or smoke.</u> (c) To breathe in this gas was certain death.

CHAPTER 8

Copy the table and write the words in the right places. Choose from: **cut, warship, second, mist, harmlessly, side, torpedo, bounced, nearest, smashed, Martian, drum.** *You will see the name of a warship in the centre column.*

The (1) _____ Martian shot a (2) _____ of the black (3) _____ at the (4) _____-ram, but it (5) _____ off (6) _____. The (7) _____ got very close to the (8) _____, who leant to one (9) _____ and fell backwards. In another moment, he was (10) _____ down. A (11) _____ Martian was (12) _____ down when the ship exploded.

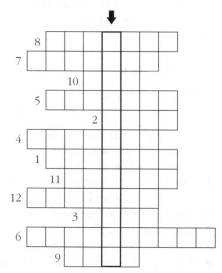

CHAPTER 9

Put the words at the ends of these sentences in the right order.

1 The narrator and the curate   [in] [sitting] [dark] [the] [were].
2 There was a blinding light   [a] [loud] [and] [explosion] [very].
3 Bits of ceiling fell and   [on] [their] [pieces] [into] smashed [heads].
4 They saw a Martian   [glowing] [over] [standing] [a] [cylinder].
5 The narrator realized that   [had] [cylinder] [the] [landed] [fifth].
6 It had struck the house,   [the] [buried] [ruins] [in] and [them].

CHAPTER 10

There are eleven mistakes in this paragraph. Can you find them?

One machine was busy writing. It looked like a metal bird with six jointed legs. It had a lot of levers, bells and tentacles all round its head. Its tentacles could reach out and hold onto things. It was taking rods, metal cups and bars out of the sphere and placing them on the ground above it. It moved so quietly and so perfectly that the narrator, at first, did not think it was a Martian, in spite of its wet surface.

CHAPTER 11

Put these sentences in the right order to say what happened in the story. The first one is done for you.

1 The long, snake-like tentacle came into the kitchen.
2 It opened the door of the coal cellar.
3 Then it picked up a lump of coal and went out.
4 The narrator turned and ran into the store-room.
5 It touched the heel of the narrator's boot.
6 He tried to hide among the coal and the firewood.
7 He heard the tentacle coming nearer.
8 He crept into the coal cellar, and shut the door.
9 It waved about, touching and examining everything.

CHAPTER 12

Put the letters of these words in the right order.

Everywhere there was silence. It was as if (1) **knimnad** had been (2) **pewst** out of (3) **texencies**. In London, he saw some of the black (4) **werpod** in the streets, and some dead (5) **obside**. Then, near South (6) **Kinstongen**, he heard a Martian (7) **winlogh**, but it was not the same sound as before. At last, in (8) **Renget's** Park, he saw, over the trees, a Martian (9) **tinag**. It was just standing there, crying.

CHAPTER 13

Use this words to fill the gaps: **ragged, inhabitants, hood, silent, pit, wrong, earth, unprepared, strips, bacteria.**

Thin smoke rose from the great heaps of (1) _____ on Primrose Hill. A Martian was standing at the top, still and (2) _____. The narrator saw that something was (3) _____. From the front of the (4) _____ hung long (5) _____ greyish-brown (6) _____, on which hungry birds were feeding. He looked into the (7) _____. He saw that the Martians there were dead. They had been killed by the (8) _____ against which their systems were (9) _____. The Martians had been killed by some of the smallest (10) _____ of this earth.

Oxford
Progressive
English Readers

GRADE 1

Alice's Adventures in Wonderland
Lewis Carroll

The Call of the Wild and Other Stories
Jack London

Emma
Jane Austen

The Golden Goose and Other Stories
Retold by David Foulds

Jane Eyre
Charlotte Brontë

Little Women
Louisa M. Alcott

The Lost Umbrella of Kim Chu
Eleanor Estes

Tales From the Arabian Nights
Edited by David Foulds

Treasure Island
Robert Louis Stevenson

GRADE 2

The Adventures of Sherlock Holmes
Sir Arthur Conan Doyle

A Christmas Carol
Charles Dickens

The Dagger and Wings and Other Father Brown Stories
G.K. Chesterton

The Flying Heads and Other Strange Stories
Edited by David Foulds

The Golden Touch and Other Stories
Edited by David Foulds

Gulliver's Travels — A Voyage to Lilliput
Jonathan Swift

The Jungle Book
Rudyard Kipling

Life Without Katy and Other Stories
O. Henry

Lord Jim
Joseph Conrad

A Midsummer Night's Dream and Other Stories from Shakespeare's Plays
Edited by David Foulds

Oliver Twist
Charles Dickens

The Prince and the Pauper
Mark Twain

The Stone Junk and Other Stories
D.H. Howe

Stories from Shakespeare's Comedies
Retold by Katherine Mattock

The Talking Tree and Other Stories
David McRobbie

Through the Looking Glass
Lewis Carroll

GRADE 3

The Adventures of Tom Sawyer
Mark Twain

Around the World in Eighty Days
Jules Verne

The Canterville Ghost and Other Stories
Oscar Wilde

David Copperfield
Charles Dickens

Fog and Other Stories
Bill Lowe

Further Adventures of Sherlock Holmes
Sir Arthur Conan Doyle

Great Expectations
Charles Dickens